HUNTED BY DARKNESS

Katie Reus

Cover art: Jaycee of Sweet 'N Spicy Designs
JRT editing
Author website: www.katiereus.com

Hunted by Darkness/Katie Reus. -- 1st ed.
ISBN-10: 1942447418
ISBN-13: 9781942447412

eISBN: 9781942447405

This book is for every reader who asked about Bo and Nyx. I hope you enjoy reading it as much as I did writing it.

Praise for the novels of Katie Reus

"...a wild hot ride for readers. The story grabs you and doesn't let go."
—*New York Times* bestselling author, Cynthia Eden

"Has all the right ingredients: a hot couple, evil villains, and a killer action-filled plot. . . . [The] Moon Shifter series is what I call Grade-A entertainment!" —Joyfully Reviewed

"I could not put this book down. . . . Let me be clear that I am not saying that this was a good book *for* a paranormal genre; it was an excellent romance read, *period.*" —All About Romance

"Reus strikes just the right balance of steamy sexual tension and nail-biting action....This romantic thriller reliably hits every note that fans of the genre will expect." —*Publishers Weekly*

"Prepare yourself for the start of a great new series! . . . I'm excited about reading more about this great group of characters."
—Fresh Fiction

"Wow! This powerful, passionate hero sizzles with sheer deliciousness. I loved every sexy twist of this fun & exhilarating tale. Katie Reus delivers!" —Carolyn Crane, RITA award winning author

Continued...

i

CHAPTER ONE

Bo tried not to stare at Nyx as she smiled at a group of vampires she was serving drinks to. He really did try. Sort of. But it was impossible to take his eyes off her. He always felt like a stalker, but he was a half-demon and unapologetic about the pull he felt toward her.

She was his, even if she didn't know it yet.

Nyx had gotten under his skin in a bad way. He'd known from the moment she'd walked into his bar wearing a ridiculous turtleneck and jeans that she would be his. It didn't matter that she was too good for him. A quality female who shouldn't have looked twice at him. But they'd somehow become friends.

His demon rippled under the surface at that thought, sneering at the word. The very concept. *Friends.* He'd settle for that right now. Soon she would be his. Even if he didn't deserve her.

"Dude, get your shit together," Cynara said, not looking up from where she was mixing drinks behind the bar.

His half-sister could read him better than anyone. It wouldn't matter that on the outside he appeared unaffected, their demon halves were in tune with each other.

After years of working together their bond had grown stronger.

Bo didn't respond, instead turned back to Nyx. To-night she had on a dark green turtleneck sweater-dress that hugged her lean body like a second skin. The heeled knee-high boots with shiny studded skulls on them were just the icing on the Nyx-cake. Watching her now, he could envision burying his face between her legs while she had nothing on but those boots, her heels digging into his back as he made her scream his name. Her taste would be... perfection. He shifted uncomfortably. Damn it, that was the last thing he needed to be thinking about.

"She can take care of herself anyway," Cynara con-tinued, pulling him out of a fantasy he didn't need to be indulging in at the moment.

"That's not the point." He rolled his shoulders once, flicking a glance around the club. His place was a nonde-script warehouse on the outside, but a lush nightclub on the inside. He owned a lot of normal, human-run com-panies, but his club provided something in the area not found within a hundred miles.

Supernatural beings needed to be able to let loose, to be themselves without prying human eyes and his place provided that—including private rooms behind a red door his patrons paid very well to use.

His two basic rules were that this was neutral territo-ry so no inter-pack or clan or whatever disputes could be settled on his land. And everything that happened between individuals had to be consensual. If someone broke those rules, they died. Usually by his hand. Simple as that.

Cynara shook her head, her shocking purple hair seeming to sparkle in the lights. "Pretty sure it *is* the point."

No, it fucking wasn't. Everyone was an enemy right now as far as Bo was concerned. At least when it came to strangers talking to Nyx.

A week ago some random asshole from her father's side of the family had told her she had a week before they tried to force her back to her father's realm. Not only that, but her psycho goddess mother had done Nyx a huge favor less than a week ago—in exchange for one from Nyx. The only reason she'd reached out to her mother was because her friend had been kidnapped and would have been killed for the dragon blood in her veins. And her mother took advantage of Nyx's kindness.

Nyx's only demands had been that the favor couldn't include rape, murder, torture or maiming. That still left a lot of other shit on the table that he didn't want to think about.

Her long, inky black hair was pulled away from her face in a complicated braid, the tail flat against her back. She had four empty glasses on her tray, but those vamps were still chatting her up. Flirting with her.

It didn't seem to matter that she wasn't flirting back, that her smile was neutral and a little bored. He didn't think she knew how to flirt anyway.

The way she was only added to her appeal, however. In a club where people often showed more skin than at the beach, Nyx never even showed a hint of cleavage—and got more tips than any of his other employees.

But when one of the male vamps laid a hand on her forearm, any sense of reason he had burned away. He shoved away from the bar and started toward her, ignoring the annoyed gasp of a female shifter as he practically pushed her out of the way. He was acting like a complete barbarian, he knew it. He didn't care.

Before he'd taken two steps, the ground shook, the trembling slight but enough that all the noise except for the music dimmed to a trickle. He had no idea what the shaking was. Doubtful it was an earthquake. Not on the Gulf Coast.

That protective need he always felt for Nyx surged through him. Using his supernatural speed, he was next to her in seconds, grasping her elbow as the shaking stopped.

Everyone started talking at once.

"Was that an earthquake?" one of the male vamps asked one of his friends as Bo gently steered Nyx away.

"That wasn't an earthquake," Nyx murmured, her expression nervous as they winded their way through the high-top tables. "That was—"

A tall woman with red hair so bright it was like fire, appeared in the middle of the cluster of tables, two feet from them. Her winter blue eyes glittered as they landed on Nyx. Her expression was unreadable.

"My mother," she muttered.

Moving on instinct, Bo shoved Nyx behind him. He was vaguely aware of her dropping the tray. Normally he would stop the glasses from falling using one of his gifts, but he let the glass shatter, not wanting to expend energy on anything other than keeping Nyx safe. Her mother was a possible threat to her and everyone else in his bar.

The female in the gauzy white Grecian-style dress smiled at him, though it looked more like a dragon baring its teeth.

He didn't bother with pretenses. He just snarled, letting his demon show in his eyes. "This is neutral territory."

She just threw her head back and laughed, the sound echoing around his club with an eeriness that felt like talons scraping over his skin. As she did all the glasses behind his multiple bars and the ones in patrons' hands or on tables, shattered.

He'd never transformed in public before, but his demon punched at him, begging to be unleashed. He knew Nyx could transport herself anywhere she wanted, but he also knew she wouldn't leave a club full of people to face her mother's wrath. As he started to let go of his beast, Nyx grasped his upper arm and moved next to him.

"You are such a drama llama!" she shouted at her mother.

The redhead blinked. "It's drama *queen*, dear."

"No, it's llama... I'm not having this conversation with you! What are you doing here?"

"I'm here to collect my favor, of course."

Over Bo's dead body. He started to take a step forward when she held up a hand. He could feel her power pulsing over his body, scraping against his skin like shards of glass, but because of who his father was—repugnant bastard—her goddess control was limited. At least here in his club. He'd had this place spelled decades ago.

When nothing happened to him, her head tilted to the side just the smallest fraction. "Interesting." Just as quickly she looked at Nyx. "We can have this conversation here or—"

"In my office," he interrupted. Because no way was this bitch leaving with Nyx. He wasn't letting his female out of his sight. And he was well aware that technically she wasn't his. But half-demons never got hung up on technicalities.

Nyx might not understand it yet, but she *was* his female. And he planned to make that known very soon. She knew he had feelings for her and he was aware that she was attracted to him. She just refused to do anything about it. But it was more than a simple attraction for him and he would not let her go. He was going to bind her to him pure and simple.

Before either of them could argue, he hooked an arm around Nyx and headed across the dance floor. No one was dancing and the music had stopped by now. "Music," he shouted, not surprised when moments later a popular song filtered through the speakers. His people never questioned him.

He didn't look behind him to see if Nyx's mother was following. When he reached the simple white door that led to his office, he opened it and ushered Nyx in before turning to see the goddess following. Her full lips were pulled into a thin line of annoyance as she watched him.

"You will treat me with respect." Her voice had a savage edge to it as she passed him.

Bo didn't bother responding. She was an enemy, nothing more. Nyx had already made it clear what type of mother she'd been. What kind of mother made a bargain with her daughter when she needed help? Especially one as sweet and innocent as Nyx? He gritted his teeth and moved past her to open his office door, using a biometric scanner with a few magical enhancements.

Nyx moved inside, a mix of emotions on her pretty face. Worry, fear and what looked a lot like guilt. He wasn't sure about that last one, but he didn't like any of them.

Her mother, who he wasn't even sure what to call, strode in after her, head held high. She glanced around his simple office, clearly unimpressed before sitting on his desk as if she owned it. She spread her hands out next to her, shoving his papers out of the way.

He tamped his beast back. Let her have the small win. Let her think she was putting him in his place. He could be patient when it came to his enemies.

But if it came to it, she would learn he was a force to be reckoned with.

"That whole display was unnecessary." Nyx crossed her arms over her chest as she stood next to Bo.

The goddess flicked a dismissive hand in the air. "Of course it was, but it was fun."

"What's your favor?" Nyx's voice was devoid of emotion. Though Bo wanted to take over, he knew that if he spoke he'd only exacerbate the situation.

Nyx knew her mother better than him. She'd be able to handle the goddess. Hopefully. If not, he was going to plan B. He wasn't sure what that was exactly, but if the female made a move on Nyx, he'd rain fire down on her.

The woman raised an eyebrow at her daughter. "No small talk?"

"Why bother?" Nyx was like a completely closed book, the neutrality of her expression so unlike the sweet woman he'd gotten to know over the last month or so.

Her mother's eyes flickered like storm clouds before she pulled a small brown package with twine wrapped around it from the folds of her dress. She handed it over to Nyx. There was a name written on it. "You are to deliver this within forty-eight hours."

"That's it?" Nyx asked, slightly shaking the box. "Just deliver it?"

A single nod.

"Then we're even?"

Her mother smiled in a way that had all the hair on Bo's neck rising. "Yes. And you are not allowed to open it."

Nyx shifted on her feet. "Where?"

She rattled off a local address, one Bo wasn't familiar with. He'd lived on the Gulf Coast for decades since moving from his hometown of New Orleans but the address wasn't familiar. He recognized the street name though and thought it might be in a residential area.

Nyx nodded once. "Okay."

"If you don't deliver it, I'll deliver *you* to your father's realm."

Nyx didn't blink, but Bo swore he could feel her pain at her mother's words. There was only one person in his life who had ever loved him and that had been his human mother. It pissed him off even more that Nyx, the kindest female he knew, had such assholes for parents. He refused to let this woman cause her more pain than necessary.

"You've delivered your message, now get the fuck out of my club."

Her gaze snapped to his, a full-on storm brewing in her eyes. No longer a vivid blue, but actual lightning flashed amidst rain in her eyes. It was creepy as fuck. But he'd seen weirder. Her power was a live thing, scraping against his skin again. He knew she wanted to rip his head from his body, could feel it. But if she did—or tried—his father would come after her. Well, he might. There had never been any love lost between them.

Nyx's mother was probably weighing exactly who he was or what he was. And if she'd figured it out, she'd be weighing whether attempting to kill him would be worth the repercussions it would cause her. Gods and goddesses were self-involved like that.

He braced himself, waiting for her to strike. But to his surprise, she vanished into thin air. Still, he didn't let his guard down until Nyx spoke.

"She's gone," she murmured, rubbing a hand over her face as she collapsed onto one of the chairs in front of his desk. "You shouldn't have antagonized her like that." There was no anger to her words, just raw fear as she pinned him with those ocean blue eyes that never failed to captivate him.

"I'm not worried about her." Maybe that made him stupid. Being around Nyx tended to have that effect on him though. With the exception of attempting to comfort Nyx exactly once, he had no experience with females outside of sex. But he crouched in front of her now, hoping to soothe the anxiety he could see on her face. He needed to wipe it away, needed to protect her from pain. It was a driving force inside him, one he didn't fully understand.

"You should be, Bo." She reached out, as if she would cup his face, but dropped her hand and looked down at the small package in her lap.

It shouldn't hurt or feel like a rejection, but it did. He wanted her to touch him and only him. He rolled his shoulders, unused to feeling anything like... this. He didn't even know what *this* was, other than the female made him feel insane with lust and possessiveness.

"I should just take it now, get it over with."

"Fuck. No." There would be a catch with the delivery, he felt it bone deep. No way was her mother calling in a favor as simple as this. Someone like her wouldn't waste it with a delivery request.

Nyx looked at him, fire in her gaze. It was one of the few times he'd seen that spark of anger and it stirred his inner beast in a way it shouldn't. He wanted to see her riled up, wild—riding him. Not the time, he reminded himself.

"Excuse me?" she demanded.

He swallowed down the instinct to order her. Before Nyx he'd dominated all his bed partners. He was used to being in control. Always. With Nyx he'd felt like he was in a tornado since the moment they'd met. She confused the hell out of him. One moment he wanted to pin her down and take her, make her his, and the next he wanted to protect her from everything and everyone, including him.

"I think we should take this to Finn, let him know what's going on." Though it went against all of his instincts to take this to Finn Stavros, the leader of the local wolf pack in Biloxi.

But the male was fair and had a lot of powerful contacts, as Bo had learned firsthand in the last couple months. Not to mention it would buy Bo time. He didn't want Nyx going to wherever this address was before he'd done recon himself. Because he protected his people. Even if she didn't know it, she was very much one of his own.

She raised an eyebrow. "Is there a question in there?"

He lifted a shoulder in what he hoped looked casual. "I was just making a suggestion. You could just run headfirst into a bad situation without knowing anything about what's waiting for you at this address."

She watched him for a long moment, an adorably annoyed frown wrinkling her forehead. "You're obnoxious when you're right."

"I didn't say anything."

Her mouth quirked up a fraction and he resisted the urge to lean in and nibble on her bottom lip. Because friends did not do that.

I don't want to be her friend. I want to be her everything.

"I can see it in your eyes," she told him. "You so want to tell me what to do and dangit, you're right. Okay, let's go see Finn."

Relief coursed through him that she wasn't fighting him on this, but he kept his expression neutral. Right now getting backup was the only thing that mattered.

CHAPTER TWO

Nyx forced herself not to look over at Bo again as he drove. Everything about the male was sexy with a dark edge, but he was off limits.

At least that was what she kept telling herself.

A little over a week ago they'd both admitted their attraction to each other, but she'd made it clear that they could only be friends. Like a complete lunatic, she was now disappointed that he was actually okay with it. It was for the best though.

She had to keep him safe from her family. Both deranged sides. That meant they had to remain just friends. If her family knew that he meant more to her, he could become a target. Now he was just a friend, her boss. *Not* her lover.

Her mother was a force of nature who cared for no one but herself and would flay Bo alive just for sport if given the chance. And her father would come after Bo because the arrogant prince wanted to mate her off to some random fae male. She nearly snorted. That was never going to happen, but the fool hadn't gotten it through his dense head yet.

Gah, she hated her whole family. Hated, hated, hated.

The only good thing to come from her family was the powers she'd been born with. As a demigod she could kick ass when she wanted to. Well, sort of. She was still trying to control her powers on a daily basis and it was a struggle.

"What are you thinking?" Bo's voice was a balm to her soul as he turned into the open gates to the Stavros compound.

They were in an exclusive part of the coastal city and the shifter compound was a gated, huge mansion behind an iron fence, lots of acres and thick trees. Made it easy for the wolves to run around whenever they needed to. Which, she imagined, was often. She sighed as the Greek revival mansion came into view, the guilt piling on. "Just that I hate dragging anyone else into this mess."

"If it wasn't for you, Keelin could be dead. You made that deal with that bi—woman to save someone else."

"It's not like she's part of their pack," Nyx muttered, looking out the window of his truck.

"Technically, no, but it won't matter to them."

She knew it wouldn't because the Stavros pack was incredibly generous. Keelin was a dragon shifter whose brother was mated to a member of the Stavros pack. So they would want to help simply because of that connection. Still, she didn't like it. Whatever her mother wanted her to deliver, it couldn't be good. Bringing more people into it could only end in disaster.

At the end of the long driveway Bo stopped behind a cluster of cars, trucks and SUVs. They'd called ahead, the only reason the gate had opened for them when they arrived, so they were expected. That didn't help the nerves dancing inside her.

"The address is a cemetery though. I doubt there's anything they can do or find out that we don't already know." She'd looked up the address online back in his office while he'd contacted Finn. They knew where her mother wanted her to go so she didn't see the point in coming here anyway.

Bo just snorted, apparently his only answer, as he got out of the truck. Before she'd opened her door, he was on the other side, holding out a hand to her.

She blinked at his consideration. She'd spent almost all her twenty-three years sheltered in an alternate realm because of her crazy mother but she'd read a lot on human customs. Bo might not be fully human, but he knew more about this world than her. It touched her that he was being so sweet. Even if it killed her to touch him.

Because even if she didn't have her family to contend with, he was way out of her league. She knew the male was a player, had had so many lovers she simply couldn't compare. Not when her experience was exactly zero.

Swallowing hard, she took his hand and tried not to show how that little bit of contact affected her entire body. She swore she could feel his touch everywhere. Tingles of awareness skittered across her skin, making her nipples bead tight against her bra cups. At least he wouldn't be able to see or detect her reaction. Unlike shifters, he couldn't scent her hunger for him. Another plus in her favor. Or she assumed he couldn't. Crap, she really needed to find out. Because if he could scent how much she wanted him... her cheeks heated up at the thought, horror swelling inside her.

Bo gave her an odd look as he closed the door behind them and even more horror swept through her.

"Can you smell me?" she blurted out, then wanted to bite the words back.

He blinked once. "I... you smell good?" It came out like a question, making her feel more foolish, if that was even possible.

"I just meant, you know, like how shifters can smell everything a billion fold. Can you do that?"

He shook his head, his amber-gold eyes flashing with something she couldn't quite define. "No."

She didn't think he'd lie to her. "Oh, okay." She gave him what she knew was a strained, nervous smile but didn't care. The relief that punched through her was potent. She tightened her grip on his hand, feeling a thousand times lighter as they headed to the front door of the mansion. Even if they would never be more than friends, she was glad he was with her now.

The door swung open before they'd reached it. Finn, the Alpha, casual in jeans and a T-shirt, nodded at both of them. His ice blue gaze was reserved as he nodded at Bo and slightly warmer when he looked at her. But not by much, probably because she was a virtual stranger to him. "It's pretty quiet around here tonight. Got most of the pack out patrolling the city. You hungry? We can do this in the kitchen if you are. You'll have privacy."

She shook her head, food the last thing on her mind. "I'm okay, unless..." She looked up at Bo and realized they were still holding hands. She didn't want to pull away. Gah, what was she thinking? She shouldn't let herself fall even harder for him.

He shook his head once. "I'm good."

"My office it is." Finn pulled the door shut behind them, motioned to a winding staircase.

Nyx looked around curiously at the interior. To the right was what looked like a game room. A few male shifters were lounging and watching something on a huge television. She didn't understand the human need for such large TVs, but males especially seemed to love them.

The walk to his office was quick and when they reached it, she gently extracted her hand from Bo's. He let out a soft, almost growling sound but when she looked at him, he was staring straight ahead. Maybe she'd misheard, but—

"You're here!" Victoria jumped up from a cushioned chaise where she'd been sitting next to her mate, Drake, as they all entered the room.

"I thought you were in Montana," Nyx said, stepping into the open arms of the tall wolf shifter, glad to see a friendly face.

"We were, but you made that deal with your mom and..." She shrugged, stepping back.

"Victoria has been worried," Drake said, pulling her into a loose embrace as well. The dragon shifter was ridiculously huge and she knew he was really old. But there was an innocent quality to him, something that resonated with her demigod half.

"Keelin and Bran wanted to come too, but my mother wouldn't let Keelin leave."

"She barely let you leave," Victoria muttered, attempting to smother a laugh.

Nyx knew it was because their mother loved them, wanted to keep them protected. A pang slid through her as she wondered what it would be like to have a parent care if she lived or died. To her own mother she was nothing more than a replacement for a daughter she'd had millennia ago, but who'd died. She was essentially nothing but a chess piece in her mother's weird, self-involved world. Nyx kept telling herself to get over it, but... it hurt.

"The address Nyx's mother gave her is a graveyard," Bo said, interrupting them. His words were stiff and while she wasn't sure why he'd done it, she was glad for the interruption. She didn't want to think about her childhood or family.

"We looked it up as well," Finn said, leaning against the front of his desk. He crossed his arms over his chest. "I haven't found much on it other than the address and that it's considered historical. They haven't had a new burial there in close to fifty years."

"But I'm going to see what I can dig up." Victoria sounded practically gleeful.

Not that Nyx was surprised. The female loved history and research and was very good at finding obscure information. Victoria was the one who'd found ancient texts for Nyx on how to control her power. That had only been a week ago though and she was still sifting her way through everything.

"There's a name written on the package. A Charlotte Bessey. She didn't say but I'm guessing it has to be a grave marker." Which was just plain weird, but totally typical of her mother.

"So, your mother wants you to leave a package on a grave marker? As a favor for the one she gave you? That's it?" Finn sounded disbelieving and she didn't blame him.

Bo shifted restlessly next to her. "It must be a trap. She shouldn't go."

She resisted the urge to sigh. It didn't matter what she wanted, she'd given her word. "I have to."

"Well you're not going alone," he snapped out, fire lacing each word.

Before she could respond, Drake cleared his throat. "I'll do an aerial recon of the place tonight. It should be easy enough."

"I don't know..." Nyx knew the male was powerful, could feel the force of his abilities flickering across her skin, but she didn't like the idea of anyone else being involved. She was still trying to figure out how to make the delivery without Bo. Technically she could use her transportation powers but whenever she did she tended to have disastrous "landings". She'd once set a gas station on fire, blowing the whole place up. Luckily no one had been hurt, but she could level a city block if she wasn't careful.

And now she realized everyone was staring at her since she'd just trailed off. She cleared her throat. "I can just get in and out and be done with it. I don't think you need to do anything." It was weird depending on anyone but herself anyway.

"Drake can do aerial recon and I'll do on the ground recon," Bo said, as if she hadn't spoken at all.

Drake nodded, his gaze on her. "My clan owes you a debt and we will help you in this. My mother is actually looking into another way to repay you."

Nyx frowned. "What does that mean?"

"She knows of your father's wish to see you married to another fae."

"How..." She turned to look at Victoria, who she'd recently confessed her family issues to—and her friend didn't look guilty at all.

Instead she shrugged and smiled. "Your family sucks. I might have let it slip to Arya what they were trying to rope you into and she said she'd take care of it. It's actually the real reason why she's not here. She and Keelin are working on a way to repay your kindness."

Nyx blinked, digesting the new information. Too many emotions clogged her throat and she had the irrational urge to cry. She wasn't used to people being so giving. "Okay, we're going to go back to that later, but for now I guess I should tell you more about my mother. If you're determined to do the recon?" she asked, looking between Drake and Bo.

Drake nodded while Bo just gave her a 'get real' look.

Ugh, she didn't even know where to start.

"Why don't you sit?" Finn asked quietly, motioning to a cushy chair next to the chaise.

"Thanks." She gratefully took a seat, even as she dreaded the thought of talking about herself. The Stavros pack looked out for each other, loved each other. She didn't want to see pity in anyone's eyes.

But especially not Bo's.

Unfortunately there was no way around it now.

Bo gritted his teeth, hating the stressful vibes of energy rolling off Nyx as she sat. He just wanted to take her away from all this, hell, to deliver the damn package himself. But if he did, it might create some loophole for her mother. Then anything could happen. Her mother had said she would deliver Nyx to another realm, but she might do something worse. No, even though he hated it, Nyx had to do this. At least her mother hadn't said anything about Nyx going by herself.

"I don't know how much you guys know about Greek mythology, but Chaos, my mother, was one of the original Greek goddesses."

Victoria nodded. "I did some research after what happened in Montana."

Bo hadn't been there but he knew the goddess had shown Nyx a mental image of where Keelin had been taken by another demigod. Once Nyx had the location she'd been able to transport there with Bran and Bran had saved his female. He hated that Nyx had put herself at her mother's mercy in doing so. But he wouldn't expect any less from the female.

"Okay, good. Gah, I don't really know where to start but in a nutshell, she's pretty much ageless. Not exactly immortal because she can be killed, but for the purpose of this conversation she's immortal in the way we all are. Only more powerful."

Everything could be killed, Bo knew.

"Tens of thousands of years ago she was... borne into existence. She mated with another god and they had, uh, children, but not in the way we would think of it. They created them into existence, just not... It doesn't really matter. One of her daughters, Nyx, died. Was killed." She swallowed hard, pain flickering in her blue eyes before her expression fell into complete neutrality.

"After that the gods and goddesses stopped creating children—what humans would consider deities more or less—so very long ago. Even before they retreated from this realm. But some of them still sleep with non-gods whether it be humans or fae or whoever happens to please them at the moment."

"Not dragons and demons," Bo murmured.

She looked faintly surprised, but nodded. "That's true. The gods and goddesses are afraid of dragons and they simply don't like demons. Though I think they're afraid of some of them. Anyway, my mother wanted a daughter to replace Nyx 1.0, as I like to think of her." She let out a bitter laugh, the sound grating against every part of Bo. "So roughly twenty-four years ago she sought out a fae prince who she found suitably attractive and then nine months later she had me. Unfortunately for her I'm nothing like the original Nyx. I am one of her greatest disappointments." Her voice cracked on the last word.

"Then she's a fucking moron," Bo grated out. He didn't like the pain rolling off Nyx. It offended every bit of his demon and human side.

Nyx half-smiled but it didn't reach her eyes. "My point is, she's incredibly powerful and while I'm her blood, her daughter, she cares very little what happens to me. You are all strangers, less than nothing to her. I don't think it's wise for anyone else to be involved."

"Well too fucking bad. Let's just get this argument out of the way now because we need to get a few things straight," Bo snapped, unable to control his anger any longer. It was as if she didn't think she was worthy of people helping her and it was starting to piss him off.

"We're helping you. And if they won't," he jerked a finger at Finn and the others, "I'm with you no matter what. So fucking deal with it," he snarled, his demon scraping at him, telling him he needed to pull back on his anger, but he didn't listen. She needed to know that she was important to him. That she mattered.

Nyx popped up out of her seat, a mix of too many emotions on her face as she stalked toward him. In that moment he was barely aware of the others in the room. All he saw was Nyx in her fuck-me boots and body-hugging dress stalking toward him like a warrior. It was beyond hot. When she poked him in the chest with one finger, he got hard. Completely inappropriate timing, but there wasn't much he could do about it. He was aware of her saying something, but all he could see was her lips moving.

Nothing else came into focus except her luscious, kissable mouth. He wanted to devour her. He grabbed her wrist and yanked her close, much to her surprise if the yelp she let out was any indication.

"I'll bind you to me so that you can't transport without taking me with you, so don't even think about it. And if you do anyway, I'll hunt you down. Count on it. There's nowhere you can go that I won't find you." His words were a soft promise.

"You are a maddening, frustrating..." She trailed off, looking around when she realized all the objects on Finn's bookshelves and desk were shaking. Her cheeks flushed with embarrassment. "Sorry," she muttered.

He tightened his grip on her wrist, getting her attention. "You don't apologize for who or what you are." He didn't bother looking at the others and wasn't surprised when her gaze snapped back to his.

The fire in her gaze was in full force now. She grabbed his shoulder and he saw her intent a second before he realized what she was doing. It was as if he'd been sucked into a vortex of rushing wind and a kaleidoscope of colors.

A crash of glass and furniture rained down on them as they transported into the middle of his kitchen. Using his own powers, he paused everything midair before shoving everything back into place.

Nyx was breathing hard, her blue eyes spitting fire. "We might be friends, but you don't get to talk to me like that."

She was so insanely sexy. Seeing her stand up to him made the lust he felt for her burn even hotter.

He grabbed her hips and backed her up until they were at the granite-topped center island. He knew he was bordering on being out of control, but the thought of Nyx in danger, the thought of her running into a bad situation without any backup made him crazy in a way he'd never thought possible. His beast pushed at the surface, wanting to destroy everything that might cause her harm.

Her hands slid up his chest, more from shock than anything, he thought. Or maybe to brace herself as he hoisted her up on the counter. He wanted her at his eye level.

But when he looked into her vivid gaze, he couldn't remember what they'd been talking about. Arguing about. All he could focus on was the erratic way she was breathing, the slight dilation of her eyes and the way her legs were spread to accommodate his hips, practically wrapped around him.

They were in the perfect position. He was tired of ignoring the fire between them. Taking a chance, he slid his hands up her outer thighs, moving until he shoved her dress all the way up to her waist.

Her mouth parted and she stared down at herself. Lacy black panties barely covered her mound. He could see enough that he knew she was completely bare under that lace.

No. No more just being friends. She needed to understand that she was his.

Using his mental powers, he snapped the thin straps. He sucked in a sharp breath as the material fell away, as he saw what was his.

She didn't cover herself, just clutched onto his shoulders as she met his gaze again. He might not be a shifter but he could scent her hunger for him, could see the lust sparking like wildfire in her eyes. The hunger is what pushed him over the edge.

Her pathetic excuse about needing to stay friends because she had a lot going on in her life was just that, an excuse. She wanted him, he wanted her. And she sure as hell wasn't scared of him. That had been a worry early on, but there was no fear from her. Just raw desire. If he gave her time to think about this, he knew she'd tell him to stop.

He wasn't above playing dirty to win her. He'd give her a taste of how good they could be together, bind her to him with sex, make her crave him the way he craved her so that she'd never walk away. Without giving her a chance to start analyzing things, he knelt between her legs and flicked his tongue up the length of her slick folds.

And knew what heaven was when she slid her fingers into his hair, moaning his name like a prayer.

CHAPTER THREE

Nyx couldn't believe what was happening, what Bo was doing to her. His tongue... she rolled her hips up to meet his mouth, even though she knew she should tell him to stop.

But she couldn't find the words. Didn't *want* to find the words. Not when this felt better than anything she'd ever experienced by her own hand.

His tongue flicked up her slick folds, oh-so-slowly, the sexy growls he made against her flesh making her even wetter.

His glass-front cabinets shook, cracked. Wine glasses started to tremble. She tried to keep a grip on her emotions but couldn't.

"Let go, I don't care," he murmured against her, as if he'd read her mind.

His words set something free inside her, even though she knew they shouldn't be doing this.

With her dress hiked up and his face between her legs, she couldn't help but stare at the way he was licking her, teasing her.

Ribbons of pleasure spiraled through her as his tongue delved between her folds. He was teasing her, turning her on even more, but not touching her clit. He had to be doing it intentionally, making her crazy.

She rolled her hips again, a tortured sound coming from her throat because she couldn't find any words.

He placed his hands on her inner thighs, opened them wider. "Lay back." The words rumbled against her, the vibration making her inner walls tighten with the need to be filled.

She might be a virgin but she knew what she wanted, *needed*. The cautious voice in her head told her that they had to stop this before they went too far, but she found herself doing what he said, leaning back on the counter-top of the island.

When she did, he let out another growl, his tongue working faster, the pressure harder as he moved up to her clit.

She grabbed onto his head. "Bo." It was all she could get out. One simple word.

His tongue lashed those sensitive nerves, the pressure almost too much now. She was vaguely aware of glass breaking around her, but she didn't care. All she cared about was finding release.

She'd used her fingers on herself before, but nothing compared to this. When he slid a finger inside her, just barely penetrating, she called out his name again, her hips rolling frantically now.

He could push her over the edge, she knew he could.

"Make me come," she demanded, not sure where the words had even come from. She just knew he'd like it.

Moaning, he pushed the finger deeper and began a beautiful, torturous assault on her clit, moving his tongue over it in a maddening, sensual dance.

When he began moving his finger, slowly dragging it out of her, then pushing back in, she lost the last vestiges of her control. Her stomach muscles tightened as her climax built and built, her inner walls clamping around his finger until her orgasm crested.

"Oh..." She couldn't get out anything other than a strangled cry as pure pleasure pushed out to all her nerve endings.

He kept going, kept teasing until she collapsed fully against the countertop. His intense teasing turned into soft kisses as he created a path down one inner thigh, then up the other. He continued on to right above her mound, his breath warm against her skin.

Nyx slid a hand through his dark hair, loved the feel of the softness against her fingertips. She forced herself to sit up, wanting to actually kiss him now.

He stood between her legs, the raw hunger in his glowing, amber gaze startling her. It was so bright, seemed even more so against his darker skin. She'd never seen him like this before. "Your eyes..." They were beautiful.

Snarling, he turned away from her, moving to the entryway before she could blink. His back was a rigid line as all the broken glass mended back together, fallen flutes, tumblers and even cabinet doors moving back into place seamlessly.

She didn't care about that though. "Bo, I..." Her throat tightened as she tried to figure out what to say, but he didn't give her time, his retreat from the room making her head spin.

She started to slide off the countertop, suddenly embarrassed by her state of undress. Tugging her dress down, she grabbed her ripped panties and hurried after him, but he was already gone when she stepped out into the hallway.

She knew where his bedroom was even if she'd never been inside it so she made her way to the second floor and knocked on the door.

No answer.

"Bo, please talk to me." Insecurities flared inside her when all she got was an eerie silence. She could force the door open if she wanted, but no way would she do that. She wouldn't violate his privacy.

Unsure what had happened between them, what had changed so drastically in the span of seconds, she tried to bury her insecurities and hurt as she stepped away from his room.

Maybe she'd let go too much. Maybe when he'd seen all the destruction she'd caused... no, she didn't think that was it. God, maybe he just didn't want her anymore.

Fighting tears, she shut her door behind her and forced all her emotions into a tight box. If she let go now she might bring the house down on their heads.

* * *

Bo's breath sawed in and out as he leaned back against his bedroom door. He couldn't believe what he'd almost done.

His demon half had been under lockdown, *calmer*, since meeting Nyx. He hadn't slept with anyone since the first time he'd seen her. Hadn't wanted to. Now it seemed all his pent up lust and aggression had come roaring to the surface.

He'd been ready to take her right there in his kitchen like a fucking animal. Closing his eyes, he collapsed against the door, hating himself in that moment.

His control was better now but in the kitchen he'd been walking a thin line. He'd wanted nothing more than to rip her dress free from her body and feast on every inch of her bare flesh, to pound into her right on the countertop.

She deserved better than him, no doubt about it, especially if it was her first time. The way she'd come apart for him, the rawness of her orgasm had pushed him over the edge. He'd never heard sounds as sweet as when she came against his mouth.

He was almost positive she was a virgin. That made him feel even shittier.

The worst thing was, he still wanted her with a desperation that terrified him. He wanted to stalk down to her room and finish what they'd started. But he didn't trust himself. He'd felt his demon pushing at the surface. What if he couldn't control himself? What if he was no better than his father?

Snarling, he let his claws free and tore them over his thighs. The pain of his flesh tearing centered him, got him more in control.

He would figure this out. He had to. Because he didn't think he could let Nyx go. Even if he didn't deserve her.

* * *

"Uh... are we going to talk about what just happened?" Victoria asked as Drake stepped over to Finn's desk to look at the map layout of the cemetery, seemingly calm about the fact that Bo and Nyx had just disappeared into thin air right in front of them.

Both males looked at her with a hint of confusion. "What about it?" Finn asked.

"They just ghosted out of your office like..." She lifted her hands and slightly waved them. "No one thinks that's crazy?"

Drake, her sexy mate, just lifted a big shoulder. "Bo clearly does not know how to act around his female. Once he figures out how to, they will be mated soon."

"No doubt," Finn murmured, glancing at his phone when it dinged an incoming text.

Apparently she was the only one who thought the transporting was something to talk about. She'd seen Nyx do it a week ago and it had stunned her then. Still did. She wasn't remotely worried that Bo would hurt Nyx. The male was smitten with her. Not to mention Victoria was pretty sure Nyx could hold her own against anyone.

Drake nodded at the printout of the map Finn had laid on the desk. "I'll do the recon tonight. Should be easy enough."

Victoria frowned. "You don't want to wait for Bo?"

"No need."

"Okay, I'm going with you then." She'd planned to go anyway, but without someone on the ground for recon, then she was definitely going to be by her mate's side. Drake still tried to protect her when he could but he was pretty good about treating her as an equal. As much as an alpha dragon could, because they could be ridiculously overprotective.

"I think I should do a single fly over first then you can come with me."

"If you don't take me with you, I'll just do ground recon alone."

Drake's dragon flickered in his gaze, his animal looking at her with clear frustration.

"Don't even bother arguing. You always lose." Finn slid his phone into his jeans pocket. "I've gotta grab Lyra and head out. There's apparently a nest of vamps in my territory. We're going to clear them out." He sounded like an excited cub.

Victoria gave Drake a smug smile. "Look, he's taking his mate with him to fight the vampires."

Drake's jaw tightened once, but just as quickly he sighed. "Fine. You will ride on my back."

She planned to ride *him* later. She smiled at the thought, even as a flush of heat rushed through her.

Though they'd been friends since last year she and Drake had only been mated a couple months and she couldn't get enough of him. It was like this insatiable, driving need that seemed to have no end in sight. She couldn't have hid her desire for Drake even if she'd wanted to.

"Whatever you're thinking right now, don't do anything in my office," Finn said, making long strides to the door.

She just snickered. It wasn't as if she could hide the scent of her need for Drake, not from another supernatural being. Finn had been like a father to her, taking her into his pack when she was a teenager. And because of an overprotective pack she hadn't even been able to date, let alone have sex until Drake. So she wouldn't feel bad or apologize. "No promises."

The big, bad Alpha gave her a horrified look before he hurried from the room. "No sex on my desk!" he called out from down the hallway.

Drake just raised his eyebrows as he looked down at her, raw heat simmering under the surface.

"I was messing with him," she said, recognizing that glint of lust in his beautiful gray gaze.

He simply looked at the sturdy desk, then at her, a not so subtle question in his expression.

Grinning, Victoria shook her head. "No way. We've got recon to do."

"After, then." The words were a low, throaty growl.

"Oh yeah." She grabbed his hand, pulled him down to her for one scorching kiss before forcing herself to pull back. Because if she didn't, they really would do it on her Alpha's desk and that was just a little wrong. Drake's eyes had turned that brilliant silver supernova, the sight melting her all over, but... "We've gotta do this now," she murmured. "Nyx is on a deadline to deliver that package."

Jaw tight, Drake nodded. "You're right."

They made it to the rooftop of the mansion in a few minutes. Drake stripped and folded his clothes with rapid precision. Though not so quick that she didn't get to enjoy his taut, sleek lines of muscled perfection. The male radiated power, all of it speaking to her on the most primal level. When he handed her his clothes to hold, she didn't bother not staring.

He was hers and she could look all she wanted.

"Keep looking at me like that and we'll never get out of here." With a growl of pure sexual frustration, he stepped back and let the shift overcome him.

She never tired of seeing him shift forms. His body transformed, growing wider and wider into a winged creature so incredibly beautiful it took her breath away. Under the moonlight his jade wings shimmered like a thousand emeralds. As he grew to full size, she stepped closer, savoring his warmth. All shifters had a higher body temperature than humans, but dragons even more so. Drake was no different.

Gently, she ran a hand over the side of his face and cheek. His diamond-colored scales were surprisingly soft as she nuzzled her face against his before climbing onto his back. He remained perfectly still, always so careful with her.

The first time she'd flown on him she'd been terrified. But she'd just fallen off the side of a crumbling cliff and had been in a freefall, sure she was about to die. Riding him now was different, more exhilarating. As soon as she settled on him, getting a good hold of his scales, he all but disappeared from sight. His huge body blurred, making it impossible for anyone to see him with the naked eye. Ancient dragons were chameleons, part of the reason they'd survived so long.

"I'm ready," she said.

When he took off, her heart jumped in her throat as it always did during a flight. Her hair flew back from her face, the rush of wind streaking over her exposed skin, making her feel alive in the best way possible.

The flight to the cemetery wasn't far. She recognized it from the aerial map they'd reviewed earlier. It had a few lights and a groundskeeper building and with her supernatural sight she could see it appeared to be well-maintained.

It was nestled next to a quiet, suburban neighborhood and it was late enough that no one would be outside. Not that it really mattered considering Drake's virtual invisibility. And she was on top of him, blocked by his body. But still, it was ingrained into her that they needed to remain non-existent to humans.

Drake dipped low, his wings going still as they descended into a short dive. Her stomach flip-flopped even though she knew he was in complete control. But when he abruptly jerked up, his wings flapping hard and fast as they climbed high into the night sky, she knew something was wrong. Could feel the tension rolling off him in tangible waves.

If Drake was worried, she knew she should be too. Whatever was down there, it wasn't good.

CHAPTER FOUR

Nyx worried her bottom lip as Bo steered up to the huge, arching wrought iron cemetery gates. She knew she should be more worried about delivering whatever was in this package, but the drive here had been the definition of awkward.

Bo had barely said two words to her since he'd told her that he'd gotten a call from Drake and wanted to meet at the cemetery. It annoyed her that Drake had called Bo and not her, but that wasn't the real source of her frustration.

It was the male next to her.

He brought her to an amazing climax last night, really only a few hours ago considering the early hour, and then decided he just didn't want to talk to her. At all. Fury and embarrassment swirled inside her, making her want to lash out.

"You don't even have to be here," she snapped as the leash on her anger slipped. She'd been hurt last night but now she was more pissed than anything. Okay, she was still hurt. She didn't know what she could have done that was so awful that he couldn't even look at her.

Bo just grunted another non-response as he turned off into an attached parking lot connected to the cemetery grounds. It was early morning, barely twilight, and there was only one other truck in the parking lot. As Bo parked two spaces down from the vehicle, Drake and Finn got out.

They were both dressed in cargo pants, a T-shirt, and boots. The same as Bo. She wondered if it was something warrior males tended to favor.

"After I deliver this, I'm moving out of your place." She tossed it over her shoulder as she jumped from the vehicle.

Screw him. Screw this whole situation. Her whole life she'd questioned every move she made, had been told by her mother and others that she was a failure at pretty much everything. Now Bo was treating her as if she didn't matter. She wasn't going to stick around his place any longer. She might have moved in a couple weeks ago because she'd wanted to keep the location of where she was staying secret from her father's side of her family, but she wasn't going to stay where she wasn't wanted.

"Damn it, Nyx," he growled, but she slammed the door behind her and strode over to Finn and Drake.

"Morning," Finn said, a frown on his face as his gaze trailed over her shoulder to Bo.

He could likely sense, or even scent, her anger at Bo. She wasn't really sure of the specifics of shifters' capabilities. She didn't bother turning around at the sound of the male's boot steps. Since she was barely keeping her emotions in check, it was probably a better idea not to look at Bo anyway.

"Is that it?" Finn asked, nodding at the brown package she held by her side.

"Yes." She wished she could just burn the thing. "So what happened during your fly over?" Nyx asked Drake, wanting to get right to the point. She was doing a pretty good job of ignoring Bo, who was standing next to her, crowding her personal space. Something told her it was intentional.

Which was even more frustrating.

Drake looked between the two of them, his gaze landing on Bo. "You didn't tell her?"

She turned to glare at him.

Bo rubbed the back of his neck. She tried not to watch the way his muscles tightened and flexed. "Not exactly."

She snorted. "He hasn't told me anything," she said, focusing on Drake.

The dragon shifter's expression was grim. "It's nothing I can put my finger on but when I flew over it last night with Victoria I sensed... something supernatural. There's a scent in the cemetery similar to a Hell Gate. It's not the same, of that I'm sure, but the scent reminds me of one."

Nyx didn't know all the details of how Drake, a dragon shifter, had come to live with a wolf pack, but she did know that he'd been held prisoner in Hell. He'd been freed through a Hell Gate. Keelin had told Nyx that after

Nyx had saved her, but she'd been a little fuzzy on the details. Regardless, he would be an expert. Still... "You're certain?"

"That scent is embedded in my brain. The similarity bothers me." He looked at Bo. "Do you have any idea what it is?"

"Maybe." He shot a glance at Nyx, his amber gaze intense.

It reminded her of the way he'd looked at her last night when he'd gone down on her. Nope, not thinking about that.

"The same way your mother and father live in different realms, it could be the entrance to a Hell realm," he said quietly.

She frowned even as Drake asked, "What's that?"

"It's not actually related to Hell at all, it's just called a Hell realm because it's an alternate place for half-demons and other beings who don't love earth, but also don't belong in Hell. In some cases they've been banished to one—"

"One? As in, there are more than one?" Nyx asked.

He nodded, his expression grim. "Those who get banished to one don't last. The realms are dangerous. Only predators survive there."

"So... how do they get opened? The same way Hell Gates do?" Which involved a lot of chanting and blood sacrifice.

"To get into one, yes. More of a specific chant than a sacrifice—though blood sacrifice will work too. To leave one, however, it's just a matter of finding the door."

"Okay." A sliver of relief slid through her. "Since we don't plan on chanting any ancient ritual spells or sacrificing humans I should be fine to drop this thing off and leave. It's not just going to open up randomly, right?"

He shook his head. "It shouldn't, but I still don't like it."

"I really miss the days when all I had to worry about was rogue vampires or the occasional escaped demon to kill," Finn muttered, his gaze straying to the surrounding fence.

"I'm doing this now then. There's no reason to wait." It was morning, there weren't any humans that she could see past the locked gate, and her time was running out. She didn't want to wait until the last minute and miss her deadline. Because if her mother sent her to her father's realm, she wasn't positive that she could get out. Sure, she was stronger than that side of the family, but for all she knew her mother could do something to tether her there.

Bo's amber eyes flashed. "Nyx—"

"I'm not asking." When he started to argue, she held up a hand. "I made a deal and I have to honor it no matter what. It's happening."

He watched her for a long moment before nodding. "Fine. I'm going with you."

"We'll flank you, give you about fifty feet of space on either side," Finn said, pulling his cell phone out. "I know where the gravestone is." He held out his phone and showed them the path they'd have to take to get to it.

Nyx wanted to argue, but knew it was pointless. Three males, all different species, but alphas were all the same it seemed. Must be something in their genes. She was just glad Victoria wasn't there because she couldn't bear the thought of anything happening to her friend. Drake had probably either snuck out or actually won an argument with his mate on leaving her behind. Nyx was betting on the former.

"Okay, let's do this." Bo fell in step with her as they headed to the arched gates.

Finn yanked on the heavy chain, snapping the lock as if it were made of paper mache.

On instinct, Nyx looked behind her, but across the narrow street was an old abandoned-looking church. No one was there that she could see and she figured Drake and Finn would be able to scent people anyway. As they all stepped through the gate, Finn and Drake moved out on either side of them like well-trained warriors. Next to her Bo was practically rippling with energy, his gaze alert, his body on edge as he scanned the wide open cemetery with bright, amber eyes.

It was insanely sexy—something she wished she didn't notice.

"I don't want you to leave my place," he said quietly, though he had to know the other two males could hear him.

She didn't know how to respond and she didn't want to talk about anything with an audience. It was embarrassing enough that he'd literally run from her after making her climax—when her dress had been hiked up to her waist, her body still trembling from the aftermath of the best orgasm she'd ever had. Nope, not talking about that here.

Feeling her cheeks flush, she looked away, scanning the gravestones. "We can talk about it after we're done." Except her mind was already made up.

Huge oak trees draped in Spanish moss lined their path as they cautiously turned down another walkway. The gravestone they wanted wasn't far off the next path.

Nyx's anxiety kicked up, but she couldn't smell anything weird, couldn't sense anything off either. She didn't doubt Drake's senses, but just because there was potentially a gate to another realm didn't mean anything.

There were gates like that all over the world, but they had to be opened intentionally. If she had to guess, her mother probably wanted her to leave this for someone supernatural and didn't want to do it herself because Chaos thought everyone was an enemy. And she wouldn't worry about a little thing like Nyx getting ambushed by someone. Well, if that was going to happen, then she figured the three males would be able to sense it. Or she really hoped.

"It should be down here," she motioned with the package to a line of simple square gravestones. According to the layout Finn had shown them it would be five markers in from the path.

Bo stepped in front of her in a protective move that completely melted her, even if she didn't want it to. She was still angry at him, there should be no melting. But the idea that he would place himself in harm's way for her twisted her up inside.

She could barely see Drake and Finn moving through the trees and gravestones on either side of them. The two males were stealthy.

When they reached the marker with the name Charlotte Bessey, who'd died in 1850, Nyx knelt down with the package and propped it against the square-shaped headstone.

As she looked up at Bo, he took her hand and started to pull her to her feet. She didn't need the help, but the weakest part of her loved touching him. Males clearly made females lose their minds.

"Let's get the hell out of here," he muttered.

"Gladly." She stood, moving close to him—and the world literally fell away under her feet.

Before she could react or even think, Bo wrapped his arms around her in a fierce grip as they fell into a maelstrom of wind and pelting rain.

It was similar to when she transported, but *she* wasn't doing this.

Wind whipped her hair into a frenzy as rays of color exploded around them, painting the expanding tornado with bright rainbow splashes.

As if they were traveling through another galaxy. Time seemed to stretch out forever but she knew only a few heartbeats passed before the vortex spit them out.

Fear punched through her as they slammed into a concrete surface, Bo turning them to take the brunt of the impact.

Squinting through the rain and wind she saw rumbling stone ruins surrounding them on all four sides, but there was no covering above, showing an eerie lavender sky that definitely wasn't of earth.

They'd been sucked into another realm. And she had no idea which one.

CHAPTER FIVE

It took Bo all of two seconds to realize where they were. He'd never been here before, but he knew it had to be a Hell realm because he was in his half-demon form and there was no way for him to cloak himself.

Nyx was on top of him, her eyes huge as she stared down at him. The wind and rain had dissipated with the portal closing, but her hair was still damp and slicked back from her face.

She had to be terrified. He held up his palms. "It's me—"

She smacked his chest. "I know it's you. I'd know your eyes anywhere."

The offhand way she said it did something strange to his insides. He had no time to contemplate it though as he slid her off him, conscious that her sparkling, ethereal fae wings were visible as well. They flared out from her back through her clothes, a beacon of light in this dim place. He'd never seen them before—hadn't known she even had them—but in certain realms you couldn't hide what you were. He was surprised she even had wings given that she seemed to take after her mother, but it made sense she'd have gotten some qualities from her fae side.

Regardless, he needed to conceal her wings and hide her. He didn't even know if he could cloak the wings, but he had to try. A half-fae in a Hell realm was unsafe. She'd be considered prey. Not to mention she was a beautiful female. In a place like this she was automatically in danger.

As she moved to stand, her eyes widened when she realized he was completely naked. Yep, transforming had shredded his clothes. Instead of his light brown skin, in this form he was a pale blue color, a foot taller and a lot broader, just like his fucking father. Unlike his father he didn't have horns, but he did share the same tattoos symbolizing his lineage. God, he loathed himself. She must be disgusted, but that didn't matter now. He couldn't do a damn thing about it.

"We've got to get out of here."

"No problem. I'll just transport us out." She grabbed his hands, frowned after a moment. "It's not working." A trace of fear laced her words.

"We're in a realm created by... a deity is probably the wrong word, but by a powerful being not connected to your mother's pantheon. You won't be able to get out that way."

Her cheeks paled as she slowly nodded. "I get what you're saying. Will I have any of my powers here?"

"Possibly. But we're here because *someone* wanted you here." There had to have been some sort of trigger set up by that grave marker and Nyx's presence activated it.

One guess who'd set it up. When they got out of here, he was going after her mother himself.

A clawing sound echoed around them, like a hundred nails on chalkboards.

"We're not alone," Nyx whispered.

"Put your back to mine." Bo was tense as he swept his gaze over the crumbling ruins. There was a wild scent in the air that reminded him of the rainforest.

The ground rumbled beneath them as Nyx moved into place, her back against his. He could barely feel her thin wings against his skin, but they were cool.

"My chaos works here. That's me," she murmured.

Creatures that looked like a cross between a scorpion and a hellhound skittered out of the darkness on long, spiky talons. He counted eight.

"There are a dozen creepy things moving toward me," Nyx breathed out, raw fear in her voice as the rumbling intensified.

He hooked one arm through hers, keeping her pinned to him, and started to do a slow turn. Twenty in all. He'd seen similar creatures before. "You have to cut off their tails, not their heads." Because otherwise two more heads would grow back in place.

He had no doubt he could take them on, but not with Nyx here.

"Uh, how the hell do we do that?"

The creatures moved closer, forty feet away now.

"We don't. Unleash all of your power. Bring this place down. Then we run." As plans went, it was shitty, but right now his only concern was getting Nyx to safety.

It raked against his instinct to turn from a fight, any fight, but he could shelve his warrior pride and run. For Nyx. Luckily he could run very, very fast.

"Okay." Her voice was a low murmur.

He unleashed his own talons, extending them as concrete exploded around them, raining down on everything in a burst of chaos.

"Shit!" Turning, he grabbed Nyx and tossed her over his shoulder.

She yelped but wrapped her arms tight around his back as he draped an arm over her jeans-clad legs. Dodging a falling brick, he slashed out with his talons at one of the advancing creatures, slicing its tail off in one quick swoop.

It wailed in agony before turning to ash, but he wasn't stopping to see his handiwork. There was an opening in the falling walls and he had to get through it before this place collapsed.

"Behind us!" Nyx shouted. "I can't stop it!"

He glanced over his shoulder to see one of the walls teetering inward. His heartrate skyrocketed. It would crush them and while he was certain they'd survive, it would break a lot of bones. They'd be weak while they recovered; prey.

The creatures were all running now too, none of them focused on Bo and Nyx. On a burst of adrenaline, he raced faster, the muscles in his legs tightening as he jumped onto a pile of fallen concrete.

He jumped off it, using one of the creatures' bodies as a springboard to leap to another pile. A rushing sound, like hail slamming against the earth echoed around them as they reached the opposite wall.

It was only eight feet high. "Hold on!" he shouted above the growing din of cries and rumbling.

Letting go of her legs, he jumped and latched onto the low wall. Using all the strength of his upper body, he barely felt the exertion of energy as he hoisted them up and over it. His feet landed on the hard earth on the other side with a thud.

Adrenaline punched through him like lightning as he surveyed their surroundings. A lush jungle spread out before them under the lavender sky. He had no idea what creatures waited for them here, but he had no choice except to find out.

A deafening boom sounded behind them, spurring him into action. He didn't waste energy looking back. It wouldn't matter if he saw how close the rushing avalanche of debris was. He couldn't afford any distraction now.

Not when he was very aware of the peril they were in until they escaped the landslide of rubble. The ground rumbled beneath them as a few giant bricks slid past him.

Shit, shit, shit.

He sprinted for the line of trees, a thin film of sweat covering him as they breached the forest. The thick trunks of the high canopy trees were a bright red, the color streaking past him as he raced deeper into the unknown. Ducking low-hanging branches and jumping over protruding roots, he didn't break pace.

"We can stop now." Nyx dug her fingers into his flesh. She seemed that much more delicate when he was in this form. That alone triggered his most protective urges. Normally in his demon form he wasn't protective of anything, his beast was more primal. But all he wanted to do was keep her safe. Claim her. Make her his forever.

The forest had started to thin, the thick trunks growing even smaller. Ahead he could see what looked like a clearing. He started to slow, when a blur of motion moved out from his left.

Three of the scorpion-hellhound creatures advanced. Without losing momentum, he dropped Nyx onto her feet and shoved her behind him.

His talons unsheathed again as he swiped at the first, slashing across one of its eyes.

Nyx screamed behind him. He turned at the sound, his first mistake. One of the beasts lunged, its talons tearing into Bo's chest as he fell back.

Out of the corner of his eye Bo saw a hooded figure grab Nyx, toss her over his shoulder the same way Bo had done.

A savage roar ripped from his throat, and it wasn't because of the fiery pain where the creature's claws had sunk into his flesh. *No one* was taking his female.

He punched up at the underside of the creature on top of him, slicing right through its body. There was more than one way to kill these things, but he'd told Nyx the simplest.

Now he grasped its heart, ripped it from its body. Ash sprayed over him as another creature jumped on him.

He rolled quickly, punching the thing in the face even as it slashed at his arms, legs and torso.

Flesh tore from his body as the thing fought him, but he blocked the pain. Seconds mattered now. He had to get to Nyx.

With a twist, he turned the beast and sliced off its tail. More ash exploded everywhere as the third creature turned and ran into the woods.

He didn't bother giving chase, but raced in the direction Nyx had gone. In his human form he might not have the same abilities as shifters, but in his demon form, in this realm, he could follow his female anywhere by tracking her scent. Though she couldn't have gone far, he hated not having a visual of her.

Her scent, like roses and sunshine, was potent, calling to him on the most primal level. He wouldn't stop hunting until he had her back.

Whoever had dared to take her was going to die. Slowly.

* * *

A heavy hand swatted Nyx's butt as she punched against the solid mass. "Let me go!" Her fists stung from hitting the man's back—this guy was like a rock.

"Calm down, you will be safe soon." The male's voice was deep and raspy with the hint of an accent.

She snarled in outrage even as fear ricocheted through her. But she wasn't doing herself or Bo any good by thrashing around like a maniac when this male was unmovable. She couldn't even see what kind of creature he was with the hood covering his head and body. She'd have to wait until he put her down.

She forced herself to remain still, to save her energy when all she wanted to do was scream and beat at this guy. The last thing she'd seen after a blur of hands had scooped her up was Bo lying on his back, fighting those freaky beasts.

Fear seized her throat, but she told herself he would be okay. He'd have to be okay. She refused to accept anything less. If he wasn't, she was going to bring this entire realm down to rubble. Then raze it to nothing.

She was aware that this was probably an overreaction of violence but the thought of Bo hurt or worse made something dark flare to life inside her. Something she hadn't known existed inside her. She might still be mad at him, but the male was honorable. He'd literally thrown himself over her body to protect her when they'd fallen into this realm. He'd wrapped himself around her tight to keep her safe. Then he'd done everything in his power to get them free from those weird animals.

"You're safe now," the male holding her said, his speed slowing from frighteningly fast to mere sprinting. The ground flew by under her at epic speed, making her wonder what kind of being this was. He was moving as fast as Bo had.

She was sure she'd find out soon enough. While she wasn't a warrior by any stretch of the imagination and her powers were erratic on the best of days, she was going to go down swinging no matter what. If she couldn't take this male in hand-to-hand combat—and that was doubtful considering she didn't know how to fight— she'd try to use her powers to at least stun him and then run.

She had to get back to Bo.

His enraged roar still echoed in her mind. What if he was hurt? She swallowed hard, shelving those feelings. Breaking down wouldn't do him any good. She just needed to get free and save him. Bo was strong. He would be okay—he *had* to be. Of course she needed to figure out what direction he'd taken her so she could find her way back to Bo.

The male slowed even more, his grip on her loosening just a fraction. His arm was like a titanium band over the back of her legs. Still not the time to attempt to break free. Soon though.

When he bounded up a set of steps, another burst of panic surged through her. Before she could figure out where they were a heavy door slammed shut and she found herself being placed on her feet—in a huge domed foyer with marble flooring.

She immediately stepped back a few feet, putting distance between herself and the hooded male figure.

He lifted his *blue* hands, palm up, before shoving his hood back to reveal amber eyes very similar to Bo's. "I wish you no harm."

The sound of hurried footsteps brought up another swell of worry. They weren't alone. And she didn't believe that this guy didn't want to harm her. Not for a second. Even if it was weird that he was the same coloring and size as Bo.

Another male who had to be at least seven feet with smooth blue skin, no shirt and harem-style pants strode out from a hallway. His eyes widened as he looked at her, then at the male still half covered with his black cloak.

"Who the fuck is this?" His voice wasn't as raspy, but he was clearly annoyed. He had a similar accent as his friend. Irish or Scottish maybe. She couldn't tell and didn't care much.

"We haven't gotten that far in the introductions."

"I don't care who she is, get rid of her. We can't have some...fae female here." He looked at her again, derision written on the harsh planes of his face.

These two males looked so much like Bo it stunned her. The one with the bare chest even had similar tattoos covering his body and arms, the symbols seeming to swirl over his skin. But his eyes were a mossy green.

"I'm only half-fae," she snapped, even though that wasn't remotely the point. It just annoyed her that they were judging her heritage. A nearby vase exploded under the force of her emotions. She inwardly cringed when the two males looked at her now with more than just curiosity.

"What are you?" the second male asked.

"None of your business. Now let me go. I have to get back to my friend." Even if deep down she thought of Bo than more than just a friend. Way more.

"The male who kidnapped you?"

"He didn't kidnap me, you idiot!"

His amber eyes widened.

"Such language," the other one with the smoother voice muttered, his sarcasm clear.

"You know what, you two can suck..." Her brain short circuited as the two watched her curiously.

"Suck?" The bare-chested one lifted an eyebrow, almost suggestively.

"A bag of dicks!" The words were out before she could stop herself. As soon as she said it, embarrassment welled inside her. She'd heard Cynara say it to a jerk customer before, but the insult was foreign on Nyx's lips.

The one on the left laughed uproariously, as if what she'd said was the funniest thing he'd ever heard.

She took a small step for the door. They weren't directly in front of it and if she could just get out, she was going to make a run for it.

A crack split the air, sending the door flying back as Bo stormed in, his razor sharp talons unleashed as deadly weapons.

Completely naked, covered in blood and ash, his eyes glowed like a supernova. Unless she'd completely lost her mind, he looked even bigger than he had in the ruins. When he looked at her briefly, sweeping her from head to toe, she saw the relief in his eyes before he turned to the other two males.

He snarled, baring teeth as he took a menacing step toward the two males. He didn't say a word, but the intent written in every line of his body was clear.

He was going to kill these two males.

CHAPTER SIX

"Bo, wait!" Nyx raced toward him as the other two males tensed, clearly anticipating a fight. When it was evident that none of them were going to listen to her—and an all-out battle to the death was about to take place, she did the only thing she could think of.

Vases and mirrors in the huge entryway all exploded at once, sending shards flying inward. She didn't bother ducking, knowing the slivers wouldn't touch her, not when she'd created the chaos. Belatedly she realized that she'd actually targeted her powers onto specific items, but she couldn't focus on that now.

All three males froze, looking at her—and all the glass and ceramic froze midair as well.

She had to talk fast. "Bo, they didn't hurt me. I don't think they were going to, either. And... look." Motioning to the tattoos on the one on the left, she took a step closer to Bo, but he held a hand out, blocking her from moving past him.

He turned to the males though, and she could see the awareness register as he saw the tattoos on the male with the bare chest. They were definitely the same as his own.

The one who'd taken her held up his palms in a peaceful gesture. "First, I'm going to put all the glass back in place," he said even as everything shifted back together.

She'd thought Bo had been the one to freeze everything, but apparently not.

"Second, I'm slowly going to remove my cloak."

Bo's body was pulled taut, totally rigid as if he would attack without warning. The other male who was shirtless had the same stance but there was a healthy dose of curiosity on his face as he watched Bo.

When the amber-eyed male took off his hood he had on the same harem-style pants as the other male—and the same swirling tattoos. "I'm putting this down and I'm not going to attack. Neither of us are," he added, shooting a glare at the green-eyed male.

To Nyx's surprise the other male straightened, dropping his intimidating warrior stance. Bo didn't move an inch, not that she was surprised.

"We're leaving," Bo said. "And you two aren't going to stop us."

The one with the amber eyes flicked a glance at the broken door and doorway. "You're both free to go. I saw you two in the woods and thought you'd kidnapped her. When you were attacked, I used the distraction to grab her. I just brought her here to keep her safe. Nightfall will be coming soon. You can go, but I wouldn't recommend leaving until morning. She is... too innocent for this place. At night she'll be a beacon for everything.

Those wings are too bright. The things that come out at night here..." He flicked a glance at her, his expression so similar to Bo's it stunned her. And he was definitely worried for her.

She placed a gentle hand on Bo's forearm. "We're not leaving." Not yet anyway. Because inside here she felt somewhat safe. And there weren't any creepy scorpion/dog creatures trying to kill her. "And I think we need to talk about the fact that you all have the same tattoos. Is that normal for... your kind?" She didn't know much about Bo's demon heritage because he'd never talked about it. She knew he hated his father and had a half-sister he loved.

Bo's jaw tightened. "It means we all have the same sperm donor."

"Fucking bastard is what he is," amber-eyes spat out as the other one made a snarling, disgusted sound.

Everything in Bo relaxed at that and while he didn't exactly smile, he didn't look ready to rip off their heads either. "Agreed. I'm Bo."

"Ian," raspy-voiced, amber-eyed said.

"Rory," said green eyes.

Easy enough to remember. Nyx gave a tentative smile. She couldn't believe Bo had half-brothers he hadn't known about. "And I'm—"

"Mine." Bo answered.

Ian smothered a smile as Rory said, "Yeah, we gathered that."

She wasn't going to correct Bo in front of anyone but she nudged him in the side with her elbow. She wasn't anyone's possession. "I'm Nyx."

They both looked at her with more curiosity until Bo growled menacingly. "You keep twenty feet from her at all times."

"Bo!"

He still didn't look at her. And the other two males didn't seem to think it was a weird command.

"Agreed," Ian said. "You're both welcome to stay here. I... we, have questions about who you are and how you came to be here."

Bo nodded. "Thank you. My female is hungry and I need to clean her wounds."

She was going to go back to the whole "my female" comment later, but glanced down at herself. She hadn't even realized she'd been cut but she had a few shallow slashes over her upper arm and her jeans had been ripped in a few places. Now that she saw the wound on her arm, a faint ache registered but she'd been so pumped up on adrenaline nothing else had mattered. "I'm fine and I'll be healed in the next hour. You're the one who needs tending to." She traced a finger down his arm and forearm, not caring that he was dirty. He was still covered in blood and she wasn't sure how much of it was his. She couldn't see any wounds but that didn't mean anything. The blood could be hiding them. "And you need a shower." And sweet Lord he needed clothes because even with all the blood and ash on him she couldn't stop staring. It made her feel like the biggest perv on the planet. Or realm.

Ian, clearly the speaker of the two, motioned to a set of stairs. "This place is spelled and protected. No one fucks with us anyway." The dark gleam in his eyes told her that was likely because he and his brother had created a well-deserved reputation for themselves. "I can't guarantee we won't be attacked here if word of her presence has spread, but we can offer shelter, food and clean clothes. We have a guest room you're free to use to shower and clean up. Unless you're hungry now?" he asked, looking at her.

She shook her head. "No, I'm fine." Nyx still wasn't sure why Bo had told them she was hungry. It was as if he was in complete caveman mode. None of that mattered though, she just wanted to make sure he was truly okay.

"I'll show you to our guest room."

"And I'll replace this door." Rory's voice and expression were dry as he moved to pick up the split pieces.

She could already see that darkness was coming quickly outside and hoped he fixed it soon. Nyx so didn't want to see what horrifying creatures came out at night. Because the ones in the daytime were freaky enough.

Bo seemed more at ease and nodded, following Ian up the stairs, his hand firmly on her elbow as they moved. The place was cold and a little sterile. It reminded her of one of her mother's homes. All polished, gleaming surfaces, expensive-looking paintings hanging on the walls and no soul.

Ian stopped in front of a door and opened it. "I have extra clothes you can wear. We don't have clothes small enough to fit her but I'll see if I can scrounge something up."

Bo stood half in front of Nyx, keeping his arm out to block her from Ian. "Thank you."

"Whenever you're done we'll be downstairs. Just turn down the first hallway at the bottom of the stairs, it leads right to the kitchen."

Bo waited until Ian was down the stairs before looking at her. "You're sure you're all right?" His fierce face was terrifyingly beautiful. Everything about him was. Even in this form—*especially* in this form.

She wasn't sure what she'd expected him to look like but he was a pure warrior right now. Tall and huge, sleek muscular lines defined his entire body. He was very much humanoid looking, even with the blue skin. Which made sense, she thought. Demons were fallen angels so if they'd mated with other beings it stood to reason their offspring would have the same characteristics. Regardless, Bo was stunning. "I'm okay but I want to check you out. For wounds," she rushed on when his eyes did that supernova thing again.

His jaw clenched tight and she knew he was annoyed, likely because he wanted to take care of her pathetic little cuts first. Well that wasn't happening. Not giving him the chance to argue she stalked into the room and headed straight for the bathroom.

He was right on her heels, actually growling at her as he threw out an arm to stop her again. "I need to check in here first."

"We're going to have to talk about this crazy behavior," she said as he moved into the bathroom like a predator hunting its prey.

He flipped on the light and since there was a clear shower door it was pretty obvious no one was waiting to attack. "Nothing is wrong with my behavior," he said as he rummaged in one of the cabinets under the counter and sink.

Well, that was up for debate. "We'll go back to that later, but... aren't you surprised you have half-siblings?"

"No. My father wants to pro-create as much as he can. I'm sure I have even more brothers and sisters." His words were monotone, but she knew he had to be affected. How couldn't he be?

"Are you going to tell them about Cyn—"

"No. They don't need to know about her until I know more about them. I don't want to talk about my relatives. Right now I just want to get us cleaned up and figure out a plan of action. Just because they're my blood doesn't mean I trust them." His voice had taken on that savage quality as he pulled out towels but nothing else.

She wasn't sure she trusted them either but it was better than being stuck outside after darkness fell. And she didn't blame him for not wanting to tell them about their half-sister. Sighing, Nyx eyed the towels. "They don't have like, first aid or something?"

He snorted then shut and locked the bathroom door. "Doubtful. I'll rinse off and show you that I'm fine. This is not my blood." But there was something in his eyes that said he might be lying. "Then we're looking at your wounds."

She nodded, tried not to stare at the way his ass flexed as he strode to the glass door. When he stepped inside she turned to the sink and started washing her arms. Her wounds were already healing and there was no blood, just thin red welts now. There was nothing to be done about this. Feeling his gaze on her, she looked up to find him watching her intently as he washed himself.

His hands were soapy as he rubbed them over his chest and arms. Her heart beat in her ears, almost louder than the rushing water, as she tracked his movements. She shouldn't stare.

She really, really shouldn't. All the blood and other stuff had washed away, leaving smooth blue skin. His body was positively sinful. Truly godlike. He was all cut lines and striations of muscular perfection. She wished she was the one running her hands all over him.

When his hand strayed down to wash his thick cock, warmth flooded her cheeks. He was half-hard and already huge. She'd noticed it when they'd landed in those ruins but that definitely hadn't been the time to check him out. Now wasn't really appropriate either, but... her mouth watered at the sight of him.

A rush of warmth spread between her legs as she imagined what it would feel like to have a male as powerful as Bo claim her.

He let out a low growl and she realized she was blatantly staring at his growing cock. Her gaze snapped to his but just as quickly she looked away, unable to hold the contact. Not when he was looking at her as if he could take her right on the floor. Part of her really, really wanted him to.

Yep, she was definitely a coward. She should just go after what she wanted, but after the way he'd rejected her last night she was feeling way too raw. Males were too confusing and she was too embarrassed to ask what she'd done wrong, what she'd done to make him turn away from her. She cleared her throat and turned to face him. There was nowhere else to look but at him so she forced herself to keep her eyes above his chest.

"So, you have two more half-brothers. That's pretty cool." It didn't matter that he'd already said he didn't want to talk about them, she was nervous. And when she was nervous, she made small talk.

"We'll see if they're trustworthy."

She sat on the countertop and leaned back against the mirror. The adrenaline she'd gotten earlier was gone and she was feeling jittery. "Is your father... does he... is he..." Okay, why had she started this conversation? She wasn't even sure what she wanted to ask anyway.

He turned away, letting the jets spray his face. Then he turned away from her completely, giving her a full shot of his backside. "My father is a monster. He raped my mother and Cynara's. No doubt he did the same to the mothers of the two males downstairs. I can't tell what their other halves are, but they're not full demons. They couldn't be in one of these realms if they were anyway. I won't judge them based on their lineage but I won't trust them either. I told them you're mine because it's something they'll understand. They'll think twice before attempting to touch you. Not that I plan to stay here long, but for the time being, you will act as if you're mine."

His words were like a slap to all her senses. Hurt filtered through her. He'd said she was his to protect, which she appreciated it. She just wished it wasn't an act. "I didn't hear a question in there," she murmured.

He turned back to look at her, fire blazing in his gaze. "I'm not asking. I will keep you safe, Nyx. No matter what. I need you to be—to act as if you're mine."

Annoyance flickered through her. He didn't need to tell her twice, jeez. She got it. This was all part of his act. "I will," she snapped more harshly than she'd intended before she changed the subject. "Do you think we'll be able to get out of here?" She'd grown up in another realm but had been able to leave when she'd wanted. Which hadn't been often until she'd turned twenty-three. Since she couldn't use her powers here she wasn't sure how that worked. She was pissed that they were here at all, knew it had to be her mother's doing. But she wasn't going to worry so much about the why of it, as simply getting out of here. Nyx had completed her part of the bargain. Now she just had to get out of here alive and the score with her mother was even.

"Yes, we just have to find a door."

"Maybe your—Ian and Rory will be able to show us to one."

The growl Bo gave her was low and deadly. She wasn't afraid that he'd hurt her, but the sound sent shivers down her spine. "What's wrong?"

"I don't like you saying their names." There was no denying the possessive quality to his words.

She blinked. She knew he'd wanted her to act as if she was his, but they were alone and he wasn't acting at the moment. Of that she was certain. She didn't know how to respond to that, but she knew that she liked it. Even if it did only serve to confuse her. The mixed signals he was throwing her way were out of control. Before she could think of a suitable response, if there even was one, a low hum filled the air.

Tensing, she slid off the counter as he jumped from the shower, barely taking the time to turn the water off.

"Stay here," he ordered, yanking the bathroom door open.

That wasn't happening.

Ignoring him, she trailed after him into the bedroom then hallway. She might not be a warrior but she still had power. If anything, she could just bring this house down on any intruders' heads. Besides, it was better if they stuck together.

"Nyx," he snarled as they reached the stairs.

"Save it! We're a team so freaking deal with it." For all she knew his half-brothers were planning to attack them. They needed to stick together.

"Stay behind me then." Frustration rolled off him but at least he wasn't fighting her.

"I don't like this new caveman attitude." Well, she liked it when he was being sexy about it, but this was different and it annoyed her. She still fell behind him as they hurried down the stairs. The humming, almost whining sound abruptly stopped as they reached the empty entryway.

"The attitude isn't new. You're just seeing it for the first time." He reached behind him, his big hand landing on her hip as they slowly entered the hallway.

She liked the feel of his fingers flexing against her, loved the possessive way he held her. She wasn't sure what to make of his statement though.

Ian and Rory were talking nearby, the tone of their conversation casual. As they reached the entryway for a kitchen, all conversation stopped.

She peered around Bo to see the brothers sitting at a table eating some sort of raw-looking meat. Yuck.

Rory eyed Bo warily, shoved a pile of folded clothing across the table. "Look, I'm okay with occasional naked days but I don't know you so put on some fucking clothes."

Nyx tried to hold back a laugh, but couldn't. She pressed her face against Bo's back to partially smother it. Awareness flared inside her at the skin to skin contact, the reaction so sudden it took her breath away. It certainly didn't help that she was pressed up against his very naked, very muscular body.

"We heard something when we were upstairs. I thought the house might be breached," Bo said, taking the clothes.

"Oh, we have shutters on the windows. They automatically close when darkness falls." Given the raspy voice, Ian had answered.

Well that was certainly something Nyx was grateful for.

"We have some food for both of you but we weren't sure what fae ate," Ian said as Bo started to put on the same harem-style pants the other two were wearing. Next he pulled on a black tunic with intricate gold stitching at the end of the three-quarter sleeves. As the daughter of a goddess she knew quality when she saw it and it was luxurious material.

"Thank you for the clothing and the hospitality," Nyx said when it was clear Bo wasn't going to say anything. "And I eat regular food just like humans and shifters and...whoever. As long as it's cooked," she tacked on.

Ian grinned and stood. "I'll fix you something. Why don't you two sit? I think we can put the twenty foot rule on hold for a meal. Right?"

"Yes," Nyx said before Bo could respond. She could feel the tension in his body, knew he wanted to say no, but these two were related to him and she was pretty good at detecting monsters.

"You're very amiable." Bo's voice was tight as he led her across the kitchen. He placed himself in between her and Rory as they sat at the high-top four-seat table. The table set was quality too, real teak wood. She'd lived in another realm long enough to know that they could get any sort of luxuries just like in the human world, especially gods and goddesses. They just willed stuff into existence and it was usually better quality than that of the human world. She just hadn't expected the same thing in a Hell realm and it made her even more curious about these two.

Ian shrugged as he opened a vintage-looking refrigerator. Retro she thought the word was. "We're curious about you. And you seem to hate our father as much as we do so you get points for that. So how'd you guys end up here anyway?"

"It wasn't on purpose," Bo said, his posture stiff.

When it was clear he wasn't going to expand, Nyx decided to. Maybe they'd know something. "We were in a cemetery and when we were standing at a gravestone, we were transported here. Like…" She started to say that it was like when she transported herself but thought better of it. "It was like being in a whirlwind. Then we landed in those ruins."

"Ruins which are complete rubble now, I hear," Rory said. "How'd that happen?"

"None of your fucking business."

Nyx winced at Bo's rudeness. She cleared her throat. "So, do you know what could have made us end up here?"

"A trap," Rory and Ian answered at the same time.

Okay, so there was no doubt about it. Either her mother or the person she'd been dispatched to deliver that package to had been the culprit. Deep down, Nyx figured it was her mother and the knowledge pierced her deep.

"She will pay for this," Bo said, his gaze snapping to Nyx's. It was full of fire and anger.

Nyx just shook her head once, not wanting to talk about her family. Not ever, but definitely not in front of strangers.

"So... where are you guys from?" Ian asked, returning to the table with two plates. He gave Bo one with raw-looking meat that didn't seem to disgust him. She realized she'd never seen him eat before, not really. Maybe this is what half-demons ate.

Ian placed a plate in front of her that looked like a gourmet meal of grilled lamb, sautéed vegetables and a small side salad. No way could he have whipped this up in the last couple minutes. Feeling uneasy, she eyed it, then him. "You just had this ready?"

He snorted and sat in front of his own meal. "Hell, no. I can transport stuff from the human realm. There's this jackass chef I take food from all the time."

Bo's lips twitched at his half-brother's admission.

"So stuff just disappears from his kitchen randomly?"

"Yep. He deserves it, trust me."

It sounded a bit mean, but she was starving. Even though she'd only had breakfast a couple hours ago, the transportation to this realm, then the running, fighting and use of her chaos powers had drained her. Before she could take a bite, Bo slid her plate over and inhaled deeply. When he was satisfied that it wasn't poisoned, or she guessed that was what he was doing, he moved it back to her.

"We live on the Gulf Coast of the United States," Bo said, answering Ian's earlier question.

Bo picked up the half-full carafe of water in the middle of the table, smelled it, then poured them both a glass.

"I'm from Ireland originally," Ian said, confirming her earlier thoughts.

"Are you full brothers then?" She'd assumed they were half-brothers.

He shook his head. "We're half-brothers. Rory is from Scotland. We have different mothers and we only met about fifty years ago."

Only? She flicked a glance at Bo, who hadn't touched his food. She'd heard talk at the club and knew he was about eighty, though he didn't look to be over thirty years old.

"How old are you?" Bo asked.

"I'm a hundred and one and Rory is ten years older."

"I'm eighty," Bo said after a moment.

Everyone was silent as they ate, eerie howling sounds from somewhere outside the fortress made Nyx a little nervous. She might be able to create the ultimate chaos but this was a strange, dangerous place and they had no idea where the door was to get out of this realm. She wasn't even sure how big the realm was. If it was as expansive as earth, who knew how long it could take them to escape.

"If you can transport stuff from the human realm, can you transport us out?" Nyx asked Ian, thinking of the male's powers.

He shook his head and from Bo's expression he'd already known the answer. "No, it doesn't work like that. But I know where a few doors are. It'll take you maybe a day to get to the nearest one."

At least that was something. When another howl sounded way too close for her comfort, she asked, "Why do you live here?"

Ian lifted a shoulder. "We have properties in the human realm but... life is simpler here for us. We spend the majority of our time here."

Rory just grunted in agreement with his half-brother.

A chorus of howls filled the air and she shivered.

"They smell you." Rory's voice broke through the silence.

She looked up to find him and Ian looking at her—and Bo glaring at Rory.

"Me?"

The male nodded once. "They won't be able to track you here, but your scent is affecting some of the night creatures."

"I smell?"

"You smell..." He flicked a glance at Bo, who was growling. "You tell her then."

Bo's jaw tightened, but he looked at her with a rawness on his face that completely undid her. "Like roses and sunshine. It makes them want to kill you or eat you or..." He cleared his throat, not needing to finish because she knew what he meant. "It's very enticing."

Appetite lost, she set her fork down. Great, monsters in this realm thought she smelled like a snack. *That should make it easier for us to escape*, she thought sourly. Almost instantly the carafe and glasses broke, water slushing everywhere until Bo or Ian, she wasn't sure who, fixed them, but not before some of the water spilled onto her jeans and the floor.

"Sorry," she muttered, moving to clean it up, but Bo stopped her and quickly wiped it up.

She ignored the look that passed between the other two males as Bo moved back to his seat. He squeezed her knee reassuringly, easing some of her tension. Even though she was terrified she'd somehow get Bo killed because he'd gotten trapped here with her, she was still glad to have him here. In that moment she realized there was no one else she'd rather have by her side.

That scared her more than anything because Bo was the one male she shouldn't want.

CHAPTER SEVEN

"I can't believe you didn't tell me Cynara is Bo's half-sister." Finn frowned at Victoria as he parked in the gravel lot outside Bo's club.

"Apparently we're all keeping things to ourselves," she murmured, shooting Drake a glare before yanking her door open.

She heard her mate sigh as he slid out after her. "I just wanted to keep you safe. We didn't know what might be at that cemetery."

Now two of her friends had been sucked into... somewhere. Another realm, Finn and Drake seemed to think. Drake was pretty certain it wasn't Hell because it would have created a different kind of opening. And *things* would have escaped. Or tried to anyway since Drake would have incinerated them—or Finn would have beheaded them. Probably a bit of both.

After all the research she'd done on Hell in the months after Drake's escape, Victoria agreed with his hypothesis.

"I'm mad at you but we're going to shelve the argument until later."

"It's my fault," Finn said as they strode up to the door of what looked like a warehouse on the outside.

90 | KATIE REUS

"Uh uh. None of this 'I have a penis so we must stick together talk'."

"Please don't say penis around me," Finn muttered, yanking open the door.

"Penis, penis, penis," Victoria chanted as they came face to face with one of the male bouncers. A ghoul named Malloy who Victoria had seen more than once manning the door or running security.

The male's lips quirked up before he nodded to the interior of the club with his chin. "Pretty quiet this early. Bo's not here though if you're looking for him."

"We know. We're here to see Cynara. Is she working?"

The male nodded, his previous amusement fading as he fell in step with them. "She hasn't done anything wrong."

"Didn't say she had," Victoria spoke again. "This is about Bo. He's in trouble and we just need to talk to her."

He jerked to a halt, the concern that rippled off him real. "Bo's in trouble?"

"Maybe."

"What about Nyx? Does she know? Is she okay?"

"She's with him." Now Finn took over the conversation. "You're coming with us too. Where's Cynara?"

"Back room grabbing stock. Hold on." He spoke quickly into an earpiece as he guided them to the nearest bar. There were only three vamps sitting there, but when they saw Finn they slid off their seats, gave a respectful nod and hightailed it across the dance floor to one of the roped-off booths.

Yeah, vamps tended to be afraid of Finn. Ironic considering his mate was one.

"She'll be here in a sec. Should I close the bar? What do you guys need from us?"

Finn glanced around taking in the flashing lights, music, scent of sweat and sex—and the close to fifty people, all who had supernatural hearing. "We need privacy."

Translation: no one needed to overhear their conversation.

"Let's take this to Bo's office then," Cynara said as she stepped out from a swinging door behind the bar, a tray of bagged blood in her hands. She set it on the bar top and motioned to a server to take over.

Once they were all in Bo's small office, Cynara shut the door behind them. The beautiful purple-haired, purple-eyed half-vamp, half-demon jerked her chin at the door once. "This place is insulated. What's going on?"

Considering Victoria couldn't hear anything from the club, she believed it.

Finn flicked a glance at the security guy that basically promised death if any of this conversation left the room, before looking at Cynara. "About an hour ago Bo and Nyx were in a local cemetery when they were sucked into a portal of sorts. Drake and I saw it happen. We're pretty sure they're in another realm but we're not sure *where.* I know it's a long shot, but we wanted to talk to you since you guys are close. Do you have any knowledge of realms or anything that might help us find them?"

Cynara's fangs extended, her already bright eyes flaring star-bright for a moment before she got herself under control. "Bo's been to different realms before, but he prefers this one. Regardless, he would never take Nyx to another realm. Never. He cares for the female."

Drake, Finn and even the ghoul snorted. The male didn't just care for her, he was obsessed.

"Do you know anything about traveling to and from realms? Maybe have an idea where they were sent?" Victoria gave her the name of the cemetery in case she knew where that portal led to.

But Cynara's frown deepened. "I didn't know there was a portal in the city so I have no idea where it might lead to." She glanced at Malloy. "We'll ask around though. We've made a lot of contacts over the years. Maybe someone will know something. I'm surprised you don't though," she said, looking back at Finn.

As Alpha of the territory, if there'd been a well-known portal he should have known about it. Which made Victoria think it might be a temporary opening. If there was such a thing. Her research was a little fuzzy so far. "Could it be a temporary opening? Triggered by something?"

Cynara blinked suddenly. "Yes. It definitely could be. I didn't even think of that but... crap, yes. And if it was a temporary portal, I can't even follow them." She let out a short, colorful curse.

"No one will be attempting to use that portal," Finn snapped in his Alpha voice.

Cynara just raised an eyebrow. "You're not my Alpha and Bo is my... friend."

"We *know* who he is to you," Victoria said. "That doesn't mean jumping into a portal to run after them without a solid plan is a good idea." Even if Victoria wanted to do the same thing.

The half-demon, half-vampire's head tilted to the side just a fraction. "You know what exactly?"

Victoria didn't know if the ghoul knew anything so she didn't respond—until Malloy said, "I'm gonna go out on a limb and say they know he's your half-brother."

Her gaze flew to the ghoul's. "You know too?"

"Call it an educated guess. When he first hired me, he threatened to cut off my dick if I so much as looked at you wrong. He didn't say anything about anyone else on staff and I knew you two weren't boning so yeah, I figured you had to be blood-related. Plus you're both half-demons. Doing the math wasn't too hard."

She scrubbed a shaky hand over her face and for the first time since Victoria had met the female, she looked scared as she collapsed on one of the cushy chairs. "Bo can take care of himself but if he's with Nyx, he'll do anything to protect her. The male simply can't think straight around her which means he could make seriously stupid decisions. My kind can get... very territorial when it comes to their mates. I'm talking worse than you guys," she said, looking at Finn and Drake.

Worse than shifters? Victoria wasn't sure that was even possible.

"We're going to get them back." There was no doubt in Drake's voice as he spoke for the first time. "My family owes a debt to Nyx and Bo is good people."

Victoria smiled. She'd taught him that phrase. "If you have contacts who might be able to help us with anything to do with realms, give us their information. We can work a lot faster if we're researching together."

Cynara nodded, all her worry fading to be replaced by determination. "I'll start making a list."

* * *

Nyx picked up the black tunic from the kitchen countertop, Bo mere feet away. It didn't matter that his back was turned to her while she changed into the clothes Ian had given her. She was very aware that she was mostly naked in the same room with Bo right now.

"Do you trust them?" she whispered, the 'them' she referred to clear.

He lifted a broad shoulder. "They're half-demons."

She frowned at the way he said it. "So? You're a half-demon. What do you think about them? Don't you think it's weird they live here?"

"I don't trust anyone completely right now. I just want you safe. And... no. Not weird. I'm lucky I have my businesses and friends. If I didn't, I'd probably be in a realm like this too." His huge body was tense, his words tight.

She stared at his broad back for a long moment, wishing he didn't have that tunic on. Now that she knew how amazing things could be between them, how wickedly talented he was with that tongue, she kept replaying everything they'd shared in her mind. Kept remembering how he'd stroked her to orgasm as she grinded against his face. And she wanted to do it again.

"Do you realize that you gave me the best orgasm of my life and we haven't even kissed?" The words were out before she could stop herself. Definitely not the next question she'd planned to ask.

Bo's huge body jerked once and she could tell he wanted to turn around, but he didn't.

She hadn't planned to bring up anything about them, especially not now, but if things went south she wanted to know what had happened last night to make him pull away. Gah, that seemed like an eternity ago. Technically it was still daytime back on their realm if her sense of time was correct, but time was always altered in various realms.

She almost wished he would turn around. With just a bra and her jeans on, she wanted him to see all of her. The brothers had given them privacy so she wasn't worried about them walking in.

He cleared his throat, but didn't say anything.

Which infuriated her. "Why is that?"

"Why is what?" His voice was raspy, unsteady.

"Why haven't you kissed me? Why did you pull back from kissing me in your kitchen? What... did I do wrong?" Now she was actually glad he was turned away from her because he wouldn't be able to see the embarrassment on her face. She quickly tugged the tunic over her head, letting it fall loosely around her. It was long and fell against her like a dress, but Ian had told her it would be better for her to travel in it when they left.

"You didn't do anything wrong," Bo snarled. His words were savage, uncontrolled and more than a little sexy.

She crossed the distance between them, gently touched his back. His muscles twitched and though it was subtle, he sucked in a breath. At least she affected him somewhat. Whenever she touched him, she ached all over. She wanted to feel what it was like to have him pressed up against her with no clothing between them, to feel him sink deep inside her. He still didn't turn, feeding into her insecurities even more. "Then what happened?"

"I... we need to find Ian and Rory, discuss the sleeping arrangements." His words were as stiff as his posture.

After they'd eaten, Ian had mentioned that they should all sleep in close proximity in case the house was attacked. *Because of her*, had been the unspoken sentiment. Then they'd be able to fight back with a stronger force. "Bo, I just..." Ugh, she was no good at this. She didn't know how to get the words out, wasn't even sure what she wanted to say. Especially when it was clear Bo was dismissing her questions.

Dismissing *her.*

Pain slid through her but she locked her feelings down tight. She didn't want to start breaking everything in the house again. "I'm dressed," she murmured.

He turned and relief bled into his bright eyes. "Your wings are covered at least."

She hadn't even been thinking of that, but she glanced over her shoulder, saw the material of the tunic did cover her wings. Something she found interesting since her wings normally pushed through everything. "Great." She couldn't even muster a smile.

Bo gave her one of those heated looks that just confused her more before turning and heading from the kitchen. The other two males were waiting for them and while she wanted to have a real conversation with Bo it wasn't as if she could force him to talk to her about them.

Not that there was a "them" anyway. He'd made that perfectly clear.

Which should be a good thing since she knew she couldn't be with him. It would just put him in danger. That didn't seem to stop her insane libido and heart from wanting him though.

In the living room/library she eyed the huge masculine furniture. The pieces looked to be custom made. Maybe they'd stolen those too, just like the food from earlier. One wall was lined with built-in bookshelves and the books to fill them. There was also a chaise and two oversized leather couches. Rory was stretched out on the chaise, a book in his hand and Ian was on one of the couches.

Nyx noticed a pile of blankets and pillows stacked next to the other couch. Ian stood when he saw them, nodded at her. "Glad it fits."

"Thanks. How does it cover my wings?"

He shot his brother a look, shrugged at her. "The material."

"Thank you, captain obvious." She'd heard Victoria use the phrase more than once and it amused her. "I *know* it's the material, but... what is it?"

"Not really sure."

She couldn't tell if he was lying and really, it didn't matter. If they were going to leave whenever it was daylight, she wanted to get some rest. The events of the day had taken their toll and demigod or not, she was tired.

"You're more than welcome to take the guest room or you can sleep in here with us. I'm just bunking on this couch and Rory is taking the chaise. You guys can have the other couch."

"Why are you being so accommodating?" Bo asked.

Ian frowned. "Why wouldn't we be?"

"You're a half-demon."

Both males snorted. "So are you," Rory said.

"But I don't live in a Hell realm. Why aren't you in the human realm?"

Nyx was surprised he was asking the same things she'd asked moments before. And she didn't understand why the fact that they were half-demons would matter. He was a half-demon after all, and he was one of the best males she knew.

Rory looked away, focused on his book. "Fuck humans. They're weak."

"They're also wonderful," Nyx said before she could think about censoring herself. They were so incredibly mortal but some lived as if they'd have forever.

Rory didn't look up from his book, just shrugged and made a noncommittal sound.

"We got tired of the human world. It's easier to fight our...urges here, anyway," Ian said.

Bo just nodded, as if he understood exactly what Ian meant.

"What does that mean?" she asked.

Bo didn't answer, just grabbed a blanket and pillow from the stack. "You can lean against me."

Hurt filtered through her that he wouldn't answer her. It just reminded her that she didn't mean as much to him as she'd originally thought. It didn't matter that he was attracted to her, that he wanted her. She knew he'd been with plenty of women. Throat tight with emotion, she sat on the couch when he did, but didn't lean on him when he placed the pillow against his chest for her.

She didn't care what the others thought of her dismissing Bo. She grabbed her own blanket and laid her head against the other end of the couch and curled up on her side, not wanting to touch him.

Bo let out a sound of frustration but she ignored him, closed her eyes. Right now she just wanted to close out everything, pretend none of this was happening.

Because in a few hours they'd have to get up and make a trek into the unknown. Given what little she'd seen of this realm so far, that wasn't promising.

CHAPTER EIGHT

"You don't have to come with us." Bo looked between the two males as they set four backpacks on the floor of the huge foyer. He wanted to trust them, found he liked them a little—maybe more than a little—but they had his father's blood in their veins.

It made him wary.

He knew that was unfair since he had the same blood, but he wasn't exactly rational when it came to Nyx's safety. He'd never felt like this before, the obsessive need to protect her. He'd always felt protective but in this realm it was at a heightened level. She was in danger simply by being here and it was making his demon side edgy and irrational.

He knew he was hurting her with his silence about what had happened between them but he couldn't tell her how he felt about her. Not here. He couldn't even contemplate kissing her here either. Because if he did, he was afraid he wouldn't stop, that he'd be consumed with the need to mate with her, to claim her.

He wouldn't be in the right frame of mind if that happened. No, he'd be out of control, just like he'd been in his kitchen when he'd tasted her, had felt her come against his mouth. He hadn't been thinking of anything else then, just the burning need to bring her pleasure.

He'd take her wherever and whenever she'd let him into her sweet body. That would put her at risk. Because if he was inside her he wouldn't be thinking of anything else. It would leave them open to an attack.

He couldn't allow himself to be weak or distracted here. Not when it could get her killed. He just hated that she thought she'd done something wrong. He'd told her it wasn't her, couldn't believe she even thought that. He rolled his shoulders once. Once they got out of here, he'd make things right between them.

"No one here knows you. They know us. They'll be less likely to attack. And she... will draw attention," Ian murmured, his voice going even lower at the sound of soft footsteps on the stairs.

Nyx flicked a nervous glance between them as she reached the bottom of the stairs. She'd taken her ripped jeans off this morning, had changed into loose black pants of the same material as the tunic. She'd had to roll up the cuffs half a dozen times. Everything was much bigger on her so she'd found something to cinch the tunic—drawing attention to her slim waist. It didn't matter that her wings were cloaked, everything about her was soft and delicate-looking. She wouldn't blend with them no matter what.

"What's this?" She motioned to the backpacks.

"Supplies. We're going with you. It should only take us a day to get to the door, but we'll need food and water. And just in case we don't make it we have a few more supplies if we have to find shelter," Ian said.

"We also have this for you." Rory stepped forward, a short blade in his hand.

Before Bo had taken two steps toward the male, Rory turned the blade around and gave it to her, handle first. "With the exception of the creatures you saw yesterday, always go for the head. Or just do that thing you do to vases and mirrors, and make anyone attacking you explode."

Bo wasn't certain if she *could* do that. He figured she could, but her powers were erratic, especially when she was emotional. All he knew was that he didn't like some other male giving his female a gift. Didn't matter that his rational thought dictated it wasn't a romantic gift, but a way to defend herself.

He still didn't like it.

"Thanks," Nyx murmured, sliding the blade into the sheath Rory gave her before she hooked it onto her pants.

Bo resisted the urge to bare his teeth at his half-brother. That wasn't the way to start this trip off.

"Let's go over the map one more time," Ian said, drawing their attention to him. Once they'd reviewed the route to the exit—which was basically a long-ass trek through a jungle—they headed out.

Ian took point, Rory behind him, then Nyx and Bo leading up the line. His half-brothers hadn't come out and said it, but they'd given him the back because he wouldn't have allowed any other option. No one would have Nyx's back but him and he refused to allow an unknown person behind him and Nyx. It went against all his survival instincts.

The two males were showing a decent amount of trust to him. It was surprising, but maybe it meant they could be trusted in turn. He hoped so. When he'd found Cynara it had been a relief to know that their father hadn't sired complete monsters, if the two of them were any indication. And he loved his sister.

Now that he'd met Nyx, knew someone like her even existed, he wouldn't let her go either. Even if he wasn't good enough for her, not with the demon blood in his veins. He just had to get her back to the human realm, back to relative safety. Then, and only then, once she was safe, would he find out if she truly wanted him as her mate. Because once they crossed a line, he knew he couldn't go back. She was it for him.

* * *

Nyx hoisted her pack higher, trying to find a comfortable position but it was no use. After what she guessed was about six hours of trekking through a dense jungle full of odd-looking trees and animals, she'd come to the conclusion that there was no good arrangement for this thing.

Even though her wings were more spectral than anything—unless she wanted them to be solid—she could still feel the pack pressing against them. It was starting to grate on her. At least they hadn't been attacked by anything.

Sure, some of the animal sounds from the thick cluster of trees surrounding them were creepy, but the three males she was with were pretty damn intimidating all by themselves. She figured that was one of the main reasons they hadn't been bothered.

They still had good daylight, the lavender sky only dotted with a few pale blue clouds. She wasn't actually sure if it rained here, but she supposed it must. Especially with all the lush vegetation.

Aaaand, she was thinking of anything and everything except the very sexy male at her back. Not that it mattered. Bo was never far from her mind.

"We're coming up to a clearing," Rory murmured loud enough for her to hear.

She turned to tell Bo in case he hadn't heard, but he nodded before she could speak. They hadn't said more than two words to each other since they'd started. This hike to freedom wasn't one where they could talk freely anyway.

But she was glad for the figurative, if not literal, space from him. She was done with the mixed signals and just wanted to get home. Then maybe figure out what she wanted to do with her life. Because she wasn't going to stay in Biloxi and be tormented by thoughts of the male she wanted and couldn't have. The world was big and she had options. Maybe she'd head to Montana, visit Victoria for a bit.

Even though the hike was quiet, and okay, a little boring, no one had slowed down once. She might be smaller than the males, but after getting sleep she was revved and ready to go. That was one of the good things about her mixed heritage. She came from two powerful lines and tended to have loads of energy. She loathed the idea of being the weak link so she was glad she'd more than kept up.

When Ian and Rory stopped in front of her, she followed suit. She was aware of Bo's presence behind her. It was hard not to be aware of the male. It didn't matter that she was annoyed with him, he had a powerful aura that refused to be ignored. She just wished he'd freaking talk to her, something. Tell her why he'd become intimate with her and... no, no, no. She couldn't start thinking about that here or she'd end up flushed and embarrassed and everyone would know what was on her mind.

Bo moved up beside her, placing a gentle hand on her shoulder as the other two males turned to face them. Even if she was annoyed with him, she loved the feel of him touching her.

"We have to go through this clearing. There are three males eating around a fire. I know them. They're assholes and they will most likely comment on Nyx as she is beautiful and female. There's a chance they will attack and try to take her so we're going to move past them. Ignore anything they say because they're not worth the time it would take to engage with them," Ian said quietly.

"Why not go around the clearing?" Bo asked.

Ian shook his head, his expression grim. "There's a huge crater to the west and a sinkhole of sorts to the east. Either direction would add days to our trip and increase the likelihood of us being injured. This is the fastest route."

"Let's go then." Raw energy hummed through her. There was no time to waste. She could deal with a couple jerks making rude comments.

Bo moved behind her as Ian and Rory fell back into their formation. She started to pull out her blade, but decided against it. She'd never tried focusing her energy into a weapon before. Not really. Usually she just let the leash on her chaos slip and things went pear-shaped.

Whenever she'd asked—translation: begged—her mother to teach her how to control her power, her mother had refused. For multiple reasons. She'd wanted Nyx to embrace her heritage. But just because her mother was the goddess of Chaos didn't mean Nyx shouldn't be able to control her powers. Part of her thought that the reason her mother had never taught her was because she was such a huge disappointment. Not violent and crazy enough apparently.

As they stepped into the clearing she was stunned by the raw beauty of the place. Sharp, jagged rock formations rose up in a clearing that had to be the size of two football fields. The odd-shaped formations stretched out in every direction, so at odds with the lush jungle they'd just stepped from. That was another thing about realms. You could literally move from one season to another in the span of a couple steps. The weather was still the same mild temperature but the landscape was wildly different.

She heard the low murmur of male voices before she saw the males Ian had been referring to. Next to one of the spiky rock growths, three of them were indeed eating over a fire. They all stopped talking, eyeing Nyx and the others. But mainly her.

And it wasn't a curious thing. Like she was clearly not a demon so they wanted to know what she was out of normal nosiness. Nope. It was more like they wanted to stick her on a spit and roast her—after doing some horrible things to her.

A shiver rolled down her spine as she felt their gazes raking over her. She was covered pretty well with the tunic and pants but it didn't seem to matter. It was as if they thought if they stared hard enough they could see past all that to her naked skin. Maybe they could. At that thought she had to actively resist the urge to cross her arms over her chest.

Unlike Bo and his brothers, these males had small horns protruding from their heads. Their skin was more of a bluish-green than the pale blue of Bo. They had tattoos though too. Very different looking from Bo and his brothers. The tattooed pattern down their arms was thinner and looked more like vines than the unique symbols on Bo's body. And their eyes were a creepy red. If they weren't staring like such jackasses maybe she wouldn't think it was creepy but as it stood—gross.

She knew she needed to keep her head up though. And screw them anyway. She was a demigod. A freaking demigod. Sometimes, more often than she wanted to admit, she had to remind herself of that. The gods and goddesses in her family had often reminded her of how weak she was, how pathetic, to the point that some days she felt like she didn't have anything special about her.

Nyx stared at the one in the middle. He had his hand on a stick he'd been roasting over their fire. The dead animal impaled on it looked a bit like a rat. Yuck.

She eyed him as they grew closer to the males, letting her leash slip just a bit. With all these rocks she didn't want to let her chaos completely loose but she was going to try something. Because Rory's words earlier had made her think. Maybe she really could focus her gift into making something explode. She'd tried before but she'd always been frustrated when she did. It had gotten to the point where she simply held her gift inside, never let it out.

"Rory, Ian," the male on the left said, standing.

They grunted a hello, kept moving. She did too, with Bo sliding up next to her. He wasn't keeping the formation and he wasn't hiding that she was his. Not if the possessive way he placed his hand on her shoulder was any indication.

The male who'd spoken shifted his position quickly so that he was in front of them. He held his hands up in what she guessed was supposed to be a peaceful gesture, but it failed when the other two males stood and fanned out as if preparing to attack.

"Where'd you get the female? What is she, human? She smells..." He let out a shuddering sigh, stroked the front of his pants once for good measure. "Sell her to us."

"Oh, gross." She lifted an eyebrow when he looked at her in shock.

As if he couldn't believe she'd had the audacity to speak. Dickhead. She glared, focusing all her chaos on his face, imagining what it would be like if his brain started melting into nothing. Maybe she was overreacting by attempting to attack this guy but she was going to go with her gut. These guys weren't good and if they bought her or any female she didn't want to think about what they'd attempt to do.

Frowning, he lifted a hand to his head, shook it once, as if trying to clear cobwebs.

That was when Nyx realized Bo was growling next to her. Full on growling.

"Female's not for sale. She's ours. Now move." Ian's voice was deadly, savage. Gone was the laid back male.

"Come on, maybe we can share her. We'll pay you for a few hours with her. My men are—"

He never got to finish the rest of his sentence. A thick reddish stream of liquid started pouring out his nose and ears as he fell to his knees. Shock punched through her. She'd done that. She blinked, watching as his mouth opened in a silent cry of agony.

Before he'd even hit the hard surface, Bo had moved into action.

He raced at the nearest male about fifteen feet away, striking out with slashing claws. Bo in warrior mode was beautiful—and scary. And she'd seen her fair share of gods and goddesses in battle mode. Usually over something petty because that's just how they were.

This was different.

The male Bo attacked tried to defend himself, letting his own talons unsheathe, striking out at Bo's midsection.

"No!"

But it was as if Bo barely felt the attack. He reared back, punched the guy full-on in the face. She heard the crunch of bone, winced at the cracking sound it made. Not because she felt sorry for the male, but wow, that was brutal force.

Ian sprang into action as well, moving for the third male who was trying to run. Rory stayed next to her like a sentry. It took a moment for her to realize he was standing guard, to protect her. But his body was tense and unless she was wrong, he was holding himself back from jumping into the fray.

A rustle of movement from behind them made her turn. Two more bluish-green males wearing harem-style pants with dead animals slung over their backs. They must be coming back from hunting.

They immediately dropped the animals.

"I've got the one on the left," she said, unsheathing her blade. Nyx didn't actually think she could take this guy on with a blade. That was her backup in case she failed.

Focusing all her energy again, she stared at the male, imagining his insides burning. Flames licking and melting everything in their path.

"What..." He screamed as fire and blood poured out of his eyes. Holy insanity. She would analyze what she'd done later, but for now she just had to go with it.

She was vaguely aware of Rory beheading the other male. As the male she'd attacked fell to his knees, Bo was there like an avenging—demon. It didn't matter how beautiful he was, he'd never be mistaken for anything other than what he was.

He sliced off the screaming male's head with his talons. Immediately the pressure in Nyx's skull eased, her energy evening out as the focus of her chaos died.

Bo looked at her, a mixture of shock and awe on his expression. The awe did strange things to her insides. She hated being looked at as weak. For as long as she could remember that was all she'd ever been considered. Being here, actually helping, fed something inside her she hadn't realized had been missing.

"We need to get out of here," Rory said as he and Ian moved to stand next to them. "Fast. If they have a bigger hunting party, fighting them will slow us down too much. We've gotta get to the exit before darkness."

"But we're going to talk about what you did later," Ian said.

Bo ignored them both, running his hands—sans talons—down her arms. His eyes were lit up in that now familiar supernova, his chest rising and falling erratically, but she could see the concern in every line of his expression. "Are you injured?" he asked quietly.

"I'm good. Promise. Are you okay?" Her gaze flicked to his midsection. His tunic was shredded and the blood was definitely his. While she wanted to take care of him, she also knew that if his half-brothers were worried, they needed to get out of here now. They could patch him up later—though it would probably be unnecessary anyway given his healing capacity.

"Fine. I swear. That was... impressive." Before she could respond, he looked at Ian, nodded, and they took off at a jog in the same formation as before.

The backpack was stupidly annoying but before she could dwell on it, Bo snatched it off her shoulders.

"I've got this," he said. "You'll move faster without it."

She wanted to protest, but she didn't want to slow the group down. "Thank you."

He grunted, cast a quick glance over his shoulder as they raced through the rock formations to the other side of the clearing.

As they breached the line of red-trunked trees a shudder raked through her. Her entire life she'd been sheltered. All she'd wanted was to leave her old realm far behind, have some adventures, make some friends and definitely lose her virginity.

And now she wished she was anywhere but here.

CHAPTER NINE

"We've got maybe one hour to go and we'll be there," Rory said quietly, barely turning around to tell her and Bo as they made their way down a crystal clear, lavender-tinged stream. "We're making incredible time."

They'd been traveling for pretty much eight hours straight. With the exception of the half-demons they'd killed and a few ballsy animals who'd thought to attack them along the way, they'd all been relentless in their trek. Ian and Rory had told them it would take nine or ten hours total to reach the exit so they should have an hour of padding at this rate. Still, she wanted to make it to the door with plenty of daylight left. Because in this realm there was only ten hours of light.

The two males hadn't been kidding about cutting it close. She understood why they'd wanted to leave right at daybreak.

There weren't any animal sounds in this part of the jungle and the canopy above them was so thick it was almost as if it was nighttime. Without the peeks of sporadic light filtering through the thick trees she'd have wondered if it actually was. Her pants and shoes were soaked from the water, but according to Ian, this was the quickest way to their destination and it helped cover their scents. She knew that he meant hers specifically since she was the one with the apparently alluring smell.

"How are you doing?" Bo asked behind her.

She shot him a quick half-smile. "Good. Ready to be home, take a hot bath."

Bo's eyes brightened with raw hunger. "Maybe we can take one together."

She blinked at the bold statement and even he seemed surprised that he'd said it. After the way he'd been keeping her at arm's length, both physically and emotionally, his words took her off guard even as they sent a rush of heat to her cheeks—and other places.

Without responding, she turned back around. Because right now she couldn't answer him. He was definitely the king of mixed signals. She wanted to ask him what the hell he wanted, but talk about inopportune timing. Not only would his brothers overhear them, but she wanted a serious talk.

The stream started to thin, the water getting lower and lower even as the river bed itself grew wider. It was odd, but the scent filling the air was pleasing. It reminded her of fresh blooming jasmine.

As she stepped up onto a bed of flat blue rocks, following directly in Ian's path, a sharp, haunted cry filled the air. "Stooooop!"

She froze, turned back to Bo, her eyes wide. He frowned, scanning the surrounding tree line. She tracked his gaze, scanned as well but just saw the same thing they'd seen the past hour.

"Come on," Rory murmured.

She looked at Ian and Rory, both standing impatiently on a formation about a foot higher than the one she was on. "What was that?" Because it had sounded human and female.

"Sometimes the creatures in this area will set traps," Rory said, disgust on his features. "Play on those stupid enough to have emotions."

Bo was next to her in an instant, a growl rumbling in his throat.

"I didn't mean she—you," he said, looking at Nyx, "are stupid. I just meant what you're hearing isn't real."

"Stop! Help us!" The screams were agonizing now, making the hair on Nyx's arms stand up.

"Bo, we need to at least check it out." Because she couldn't walk away from that gut-wrenching cry. She simply couldn't.

Rory and Ian stepped back to them, indecision on their faces. Which meant they weren't sure the cries were fake either.

"That sounds real," she murmured as another cry, this one weaker, cut through the air.

They all looked to the east, in the direction of the fading cry.

"We shouldn't get off the path..." Rory trailed off, not even sounding convinced of his own words.

Nyx didn't care what they thought, but she did care about Bo's opinion. "What if it's a female in trouble and we do nothing?" Because half-demon or not, Bo respected women. It was one of the things that had drawn her to him originally. He adored his sister and now that she knew what had happened to his mother, it made sense.

Jaw clenched tight, he looked at his half-brothers. "Can you walk away from females potentially in trouble?"

Their answer would tell Nyx everything she needed to know about them. To her relief, both males shook their heads, Rory letting out a curse. Instead of continuing down the stream, they moved toward the woods. They all spread out, though Bo stayed right next to her.

"Look for traps on the ground or in the trees," Ian warned as they moved.

Nyx's heart beat a staccato tattoo against her chest as her feet sank into the mushy ground. She ignored the gross feeling of mud and whatever else that squished into her shoes and between her toes.

The farther they walked through the forest, the more the trees started to thin and definite male voices filled the air. And females crying.

Worry hummed through Nyx. From what she knew this wasn't a place for females of any species. She glanced at Bo and saw the same concern etched on his sharp features. Shelving all her mixed emotions right now, she reached out and grabbed his hand, linking her fingers through his.

His eyes widened, but he simply squeezed her hand, held tight. The feel of him grounded her, eased her fear of whatever was through those trees. The louder the voices and laughter grew, the four of them slowed and Ian and Rory moved toward them with an incredible stealth.

She could see smoke and sunlight through the thinning trees, but it was still darker under the awning of foliage.

As the two males reached them, Rory made a bunch of hand signals she took to mean they should wait while he did some recon. It was clear Bo and Ian didn't like it, and neither did she, but it made more sense for one of them to scout as opposed to all of them. And the brothers had way more knowledge of this realm than Bo or her.

After they all nodded, Rory slid through the trees like a wraith, seeming to blend with the shadows.

Blood rushed in her ears as the seconds turned into minutes. Bo never let go of her hand as they scanned the trees, waiting and watching. It was as if an eternity passed but Rory was back in less than ten minutes, his expression grim as he hurried toward them.

"It's an old castle, mostly ruins. Koighans are running it. Three female captives. One is in the leader's quarters, two are in cages. The ones in the cages look like they've been there a while." He swallowed hard, his jaw clenched tight as he looked at his brother. They seemed to be having some sort of wordless conversation.

"So what's the plan?" Bo asked quietly, interrupting their non-conversation.

"The female in the leader's quarters is in bad shape, but I think we can get her out undetected. At least for a little while. The only way we'll get the other two free is with a distraction."

"How do we do that?" Nyx looked between them. Her battle tactics were pretty much nil, but she could create some havoc. "Should I bring down a wall of the ruins?"

"Yes..." Rory trailed off, looking at Bo warily. "That might work. There's only one thing that will distract all of them completely."

"No." Bo didn't raise his voice, but the savagery in that one word was unmistakable.

She frowned. "What is it?"

"You."

CHAPTER TEN

Victoria linked her fingers through Drake's as they strode down the cobbled streets of the Quarter. Even though they were a few blocks back, they had a perfect view of the back façade of St. Louis Cathedral in the distance. It was one of the oldest cathedrals in the United States and she'd been in it many times over the years. Unfortunately they weren't in New Orleans to visit, but to see a magic man.

"I don't like going in here without any recon." Drake glanced around the street they were headed down.

Vehicles lined the curb and a few people strolled down the sidewalks, but not many. A Clydesdale horse pulling a small buggy with no customers in the back clomped past them. The driver nodded once, slightly tipping his hat. She smiled back. There was a parade in another part of the Quarter so they'd gotten lucky that there wasn't much traffic this time of day. There were a few shops and cafes nearby but mainly it was a residential street, which also helped.

"I've been there before. The owner is human and a sweet old man." Well, maybe sweet was a stretch, but Thurman had always been kind to her. So when Cynara had gotten a tip about someone who owned a magic shop losing a wormhole spell in New Orleans, Victoria had known where to go. There were plenty of magic shops in New Orleans, many real, but Thurman's was the most likely to have something along the line of a wormhole spell.

"How does one even *lose* a spell?" Drake frowned, his handsome face the picture of frustration.

"The man is human and I think in his seventies. Or close to it by now." It bothered Victoria though. Thurman was known for being careful. He'd always hired shifters or vamps for extra security at his shop. He was definitely human, but there was a little more to him. She'd never pressed, but his ability to wield magic was inborn, that much she was certain of.

"We should have just let Cynara come here instead."

"Whining isn't sexy," she murmured, nudging him with her hip.

He shot her a sideways look, his dragon flashing in his eyes. "I do not whine."

She leaned her head against his shoulder, grinning. "That's up for debate. And Cynara was too wired. She's worried about her brother. Granted so are we, but she's more likely to attack and kill him, or get herself ashed by this magic man if she comes in fangs blazing. It's better for us to be here, especially since he knows me." It had been about two years since she'd been here though.

Drake just made a grunting sound, probably muttering about his stubborn mate.

"Here," she said, motioning to an iron gate off the sidewalk. She groaned when she saw the heavy lock in place. The shop didn't have a website and no one had answered when she'd called earlier. It had kept ringing and ringing. She peered through the bars, able to see only lush plants spilling over an arched entryway. She could hear running water and remembered he had a fountain in the garden past the archway as well. His shop was beyond the courtyard but not visible from the sidewalk.

Drake grasped the lock, pulled. It snapped off as if it were made of plastic.

"Drake," she whispered, looking around. There was a couple across the street walking their dog and a woman wearing spiky boots headed their way along the side-walk. No one was paying attention to them, but still, she felt bad.

He just shrugged and pushed the gate open. It creaked as he stepped through, doing a full scan of the archway, definitely looking for traps.

When he was certain they were okay, he nodded once and held back for her hand without looking at her. Her heart warmed at the way he automatically reached for her. She was always doing that to him too. It was like breathing now. The need to touch him, to hold him, it was something she'd never tire of. "I don't scent any-thing off," she murmured. No other supernatural crea-tures at least.

"Me neither." But Drake was still tense, his big body vibrating with energy as they strode through to the garden area.

To Victoria's surprise Thurman was sitting at a round iron table with a ceramic tray, a teapot and small cup in front of him. He wore a gray three piece suit with a burgundy tie and a tan bowler hat. As always his pocket watch chain dangled from his vest.

"I'm closed for business," he murmured, flicking a dismissive glance in their direction. But he smiled when he saw her, his teeth blindingly white against his ebony skin. "Victoria." He set his cup down and stood in that regal way of his. "It's been years."

Thankful he remembered her, she smiled and strode toward him. Drake lightly grasped her elbow and let out a soft growl. Though she wanted to be annoyed, she knew her mate simply wanted to protect her. Instead of moving forward and hugging Thurman, she slid her arm around Drake's waist.

"Thurman, this is my mate, Drake."

His lips quirked as he nodded once politely. "I can see that." When he eyed Drake there was a touch of awe in his eyes. "Never thought I'd get to meet one of your kind before I leave this plane."

Drake flicked a look at Victoria before he turned back to Thurman. "You know what I am?"

"Your kinds has many names, but I can see you are a dragon."

Victoria noted the way he said see, not know. Drake did too.

"You can *see?*" Drake's voice had gone dangerously quiet.

This was definitely news to her. If she'd known he had whatever capability this was, she wouldn't have brought her mate. In the past she'd come here for herbs whenever she was in town. Even though she was a healer she still used natural healing methods because she couldn't afford to burn herself out by using her healing energy alone.

Thurman frowned as though surprised. "I thought you knew I was a seer."

Victoria shook her head.

He shifted uncomfortably. "Ah, well. I am. Would you like to sit?"

"Yes, thank you." She nudged Drake's side when he stood there like a statue. She could feel the annoyance rolling off him.

She understood. It was jarring for a human to be able to see what they were, especially when shifters guarded their true selves carefully. But there was nothing they could do about it. When Thurman offered them tea, they both declined.

Instead of sitting, Drake stood at her back when she sat on one of the wrought iron chairs. "How have you been?" she asked, leaning back casually even though she felt anything but that right now. Her shifter senses had always trusted Thurman and she knew her wolf was more attuned to people than she was. That hadn't changed, it was just different now that she knew he could *see* her true self.

"Well enough. But you don't want to talk about that. What brings you here?"

She cleared her throat. "I did try to call."

"I've been… taking a break from business. My shop was robbed. Not the first time, but…" He trailed off, lifting a shoulder.

She could see the robbery bothered him. "Were you here when it happened?"

"I… don't know. I've had a lapse in memory. So have my staff."

She looked up at her mate. His expression was dark. "Or more likely, someone erased your memory. Was a wormhole package stolen?"

Yep, that was Drake, right to the point.

Thurman blinked once. "That's why you're here." Not a question.

She nodded.

He rubbed the back of his neck, nodded. "Among a couple other things. I didn't notice at first, but one evening a week ago is a complete blank. I woke up at home, in my bed. My vampire assistant experienced the same thing that night."

"Security—"

"Security feeds were all wiped," he said, cutting Drake off. "You know who did this to me?" His expression turned dark, deadly.

"Unfortunately no. Some friends of ours were sucked into a... vortex or wormhole." Victoria wasn't certain if the terms were interchangeable. "Your spell, what are the parameters of it?" she continued. Magic wasn't remotely her specialty.

"The spell can be used to open a door to another realm. Instead of a blood sacrifice or having to know a specific chant, the spell does the job for you."

"So anyone can open a door with a spell?" Drake growled.

"No. There has to be a trigger. And I can't answer what the trigger might be because I don't know who took it and I don't know how they...formatted it, so to speak. Do you have an idea who stole from me?" Anger burned bright in his gaze.

"We're still trying to figure that out. Whoever did it... let it go," Drake said softly. "They're powerful."

Victoria reached back and patted the hand Drake had set on her shoulder. She was glad he'd told Thurman to let it go. Whoever had taken from him and then set up Nyx and Bo had to be incredibly powerful. Wiping someone's memory was a very, very difficult feat. Most supernatural beings were immune to something like that, but humans weren't. Apparently not even a magic man. And he'd said his vampire assistant had a memory loss as well.

It made Victoria even more worried about who'd sent Nyx and Bo to a Hell realm. Whoever had done it had been careful to cover their tracks. The fact that they hadn't killed Thurman or his assistant when they likely could have, was the only thing that eased Victoria's mind. But not by much.

She needed to find her friends. And fast.

* * *

Bo resisted the urge to let his talons unsheathe, to swipe his brother's head off at the suggestion that they were letting Nyx walk into that Koighan camp. "No. Fucking. Way." The only reason he wasn't roaring right now was because they couldn't afford anyone to hear them.

He knew what Koighans were. Inbred half-demons. True monsters who only cared about killing and receiving pleasure at any cost. They almost never came to the human realm but on the off chance one did, they were loathed and hunted by all supernatural beings. He wouldn't let them in his club. Hell, he'd kill one on sight.

"What do you mean?" Nyx asked, completely ignoring Bo.

He growled at her and she continued to ignore him.

Rory lifted a shoulder. "I walk in there with you as if I want to sell you. If your wings are showing, it will bring everyone from the camp to see, except maybe a few guards. Bo and Ian can free the females."

"First, you're not taking Nyx in there. Second, say on some hypothetical insane plane of existence I allow this shit to go down, how would you and Nyx get out? You wouldn't. Because if you say you won't sell her, they'll kill you and take her. You know what these bastards are like." Bo was vibrating with rage, could feel his eyes glowing, heating up with the force of his internal rage. He was barely keeping himself in check, barely suppressing his need to kill, to destroy everything in his path that was a threat to Nyx.

Nyx pulled her hand from his, her expression a mix of too many things for him to decipher. Probably because he could barely see past his rage.

"You don't *allow* me to do anything. No one does. I'm my own person." She looked away from him then, hurt clear on her face as she turned to Rory.

He knew why, or at least guessed. Her family treated her like a chess piece, as an object. But he would never do that. He just needed her safe.

"That's where your gift would come in. But without knowing the extent of it, I don't know if this is a viable plan or not. Once the females are free, you and I would have a very limited window to attack and escape. I know I can take on at least ten of them, but with you..." He shook his head. "It's not ideal circumstances. What exactly can you do?"

"Well, you saw what I did to those two males. I can also bring down pretty much any physical structure, but until very recently my gifts haven't been very focused."

That being an understatement. They hadn't had a chance to talk about how she'd killed those two males earlier. Bo might have delivered the final blow to one of them, but Nyx had already killed the male... with her mind. He wasn't sure what she'd done exactly. He wasn't sure if she could do it again.

"There's no guarantee you'll be able to focus your energy now. Especially not if your emotions are high." Somehow Bo kept his voice even when all he wanted to do was sling her over his shoulder caveman-style and get her to safety.

"We can't walk away from this. What if that was me in there? Or your mother?" Yeah, she was playing on the sympathy card. "Or Cynara?"

He noticed she didn't flat out say "his sister" but there was a certain desperation in her voice. Under any other circumstance he wouldn't even think twice about walking away. Even now he didn't *want* to. He didn't doubt his ability to fight the fuckers in that camp. But the need to keep Nyx safe from everything was a living thing inside him, dark and feral. Deep down he knew that if he resisted this, that if he did what his primal instinct said and just whisked Nyx away, that she'd hate him for it in the end. She had a strong moral code, something he'd seen in the most subtle of ways before. He admired it. She needed a male who was good enough for her. While he knew he'd never be good enough, he had to try to do the right thing.

Unable to contain all of his anger, his talons unsheathed by his side. "I'm the one who walks into the camp with you."

Both Rory and Ian shook their heads. "No," Ian said. "One of us has to do it. They *know* us. If you walk in with her they're more likely to attack first and just take her. You're a stranger. And even if they let you in past the first layer of guards, the moment one of them looks at Nyx wrong, you'll lose your shit."

Bo wanted to deny it, but there was no way he could because it was the truth. He rolled his shoulders once, easing back from the urge to lash out. "So these fuckers know you. How?"

"They encroached on our territory and we killed a few dozen of them. Years ago. I didn't even know there was a band of them in this realm anymore."

Nyx's head tilted to the side a fraction. "Wouldn't that stand to reason they'd just attack you?"

"No. They fear strength. Besides, if it's just me entering their camp they won't attack straight off because they'll want to know where Ian is. He killed more of them than me. And, no offense," he said, shooting a quick glance at Bo before looking back at her, "they'll listen to me if you're with me for the sole fact that you're... attractive."

Bo could tell Rory's first instinct was to say something crasser. He was glad the male hadn't. Would save Bo the trouble of smashing his fist into the guy's face later. He rolled his shoulders again. Fuck. He couldn't be contemplating this. He absolutely couldn't. If anything happened to Nyx he didn't know how he'd forgive himself.

But when he looked at Nyx, saw the determined set of her jaw, he knew this was happening. "You're going to draw a map of the place, then we're going to go over everything. And you will defend her with your life." It wasn't a question. And the not-so-underlying threat in Bo's voice said that if Rory didn't, Bo would end the male's life.

They moved back deeper into the woods and after Bo was as satisfied as he'd ever be that this had a chance of working, he nodded at his half-brothers. If they timed this right they'd be able to save the females, kill the half-demons and make it to the exit of this realm by the time darkness fell—ish. They'd be cutting it close, but it would have to do.

"All you have to do now is change," Ian said, turning his back to Nyx to give her privacy. Rory immediately did the same.

Nyx looked at Bo, raised an eyebrow. He read the silent question or maybe order in that clear gaze. She thought he should turn around. Fuck that.

He crossed his arms over his chest. He wasn't chivalrous, was barely civilized some days. If his female was taking off her clothes, he was watching.

Nyx looked a little nervous but also a lot freaking brave as she defiantly stripped her tunic off and put on her dingy, torn filmy top she'd had on when they'd first arrived here. Her wings flared bright, the intricate designs on the ethereal wisps floating out behind her immediately drawing the eye.

Which was the point. To infiltrate and distract, they needed the ultimate distraction. A fae. Those monsters wouldn't know she was half-fae. Wouldn't care. They'd just see pretty, delicate prey.

He swallowed back his fear. He'd spent most of his life without that emotion but now... he grabbed Nyx by the hips, tugged her to him and crushed his mouth to hers. He was an undeserving bastard who couldn't, in a billion years, ever deserve this female, but he was damn sure going to try. After they got out of here he needed to convince her to mate with him. He knew shifter males courted their females. He could do that. Originally he'd planned to tie her to him with really good sex. Now he knew he needed to prove his worth to her, show her he could protect her, treat her as an equal. It was what she deserved.

Feeling primal, hungry, he flicked his tongue against hers in a brief mating, his strokes demanding. The feel of her mouth against his, her tongue tentative, sweet and exploring smoothed out something dark inside him. It pushed back that edge of insanity he'd been riding and he had no idea how that was even possible.

He forced himself to pull back, knew he had to do it now or he'd never let her go. He'd just take her and leave and deal with her anger later. But he couldn't do that to her. He had to respect her decision, respect *her*... and her power. In this place her energy wasn't as cloaked as it had been in the human realm. And ever since she'd killed those half-demons he sensed it even more, pulsing against his skin. She was a strong woman.

He had to let her do this, be part of this. Even if it killed him. "You're coming back to me," he ordered. Because it wasn't even a question. She *would* come back. He wouldn't live in a world without her.

Something flickered in her gaze, something he couldn't define, even if he liked it at the most primal level. "I will."

* * *

Nyx walked a foot behind Rory, feeling more exposed than she'd ever been. It didn't matter that she had on clothes, her *wings* were showing. It was like she had invisible neon arrows above her head pointing at her saying "look at me, look at me!" She knew it was for the best that Bo wasn't with her, but she still wished he was. Especially after the way he'd just kissed her, just told her she was coming back to him. There'd been something in his tone that felt as possessive as his kiss had been. Which gave her hope that maybe he wanted more with her.

She flicked her wings, the action a nervous habit. She could solidify them if she wanted, but in this spectral form, no one could hurt her wings. Since she wasn't sure what these Koighans would do when they saw her, she was keeping them ethereal.

Bo and Ian would be moving around to the back of the camp within minutes of her and Rory entering. At least that was the plan. And she had complete faith in Bo. No matter what, he wouldn't let anything happen to her. *She* didn't plan on letting anything happen to herself or them. Even though she didn't know them well, she was starting to feel a sense of protectiveness for Rory and Ian. The two males hadn't needed to help them. They could have sent her and Bo off into the wild with a map and nothing else. Instead they'd offered them shelter last night, come with them and even now they were helping captives simply because they could. It was hard not to like males like that.

Instead of feeling weaker after the long trek today and killing those two males she was still pulsing with energy. It hummed in her, as if she'd woken something inside. She'd even tried to transport on the off chance she'd gotten her ability back, but no such luck. She couldn't wait to get out of this realm, to talk to Bo about everything. Her lips were still tingling from his claiming, and that was exactly what that kiss had been. She felt it bone deep. Even if he didn't realize it. She just hoped he would man up and stop pushing her away.

The path into the camp was a trail of uneven round stones. They passed through the broken-down ruins of what had likely once been a small castle. Or maybe just a fortress. She'd seen some truly great castles and this didn't look like much. In the distance, between more falling-down pillars of stone, she could see two cages suspended in the air. It was difficult to tell because it was in the back part of the "castle", but she could see a body in each.

Swallowing hard, she looked at the back of Rory's head, focused on him. She forced herself to ignore how quiet it had gotten now that she and Rory were inside the ruins. She ignored the way two yellowish-colored males with razor-sharp teeth and scaly bodies inched closer to her.

"Don't touch my merchandise." Rory didn't raise his voice as he turned to look at the males, but he did bare his...canines. Well that was interesting. She'd assumed he was half-demon, half-human. But maybe he was a shifter of some sort.

The males held up their hands as if they hadn't been planning that at all, but they both leered at her, their lust clear and disgusting.

"I'll enjoy fucking you later," the closest said, the stench of his breath so overwhelming she gagged once as he flicked his extra-long, snakelike tongue at her.

A measure of fear slid through her veins, but at the same time, anger punched through her. Yeah, maybe it was arrogant, but she was a freaking demigod. She was the daughter of Chaos and a fae prince. And this male thought he could talk to her that way?

She looked away from him, not bothering to respond. Instead she imagined his ankle snapping completely in half, the bone shoving through his skin in the most painful way possible.

"Agh!" The male shouted in pain but she didn't turn around to see her handiwork.

"What the fuck? You forget how to walk?" A male howled in laughter, clearly uncaring about his friend's injury.

Rory flicked a glance over his shoulder, looked past her, then down at her. His mossy green eyes were bright with amusement, and a little respect, as he turned around. "Showtime," he murmured, quiet enough for her ears only.

Nyx kept walking, but peeked around him to see twenty males walking their way, one leading the pack.

The male in the front was about half a foot taller than the rest. He had the same yellowish skin and reptilian features. Just like the first two males, this group wore what amounted to loin cloths and boots. Their scaly skin shimmered under the fading sunlight. Another reminder that their time was limited. They needed to save these females and get out alive.

"Wolf-demon," the leader greeted Rory.

Nyx internally frowned at the name, but kept her expression as neutral as possible. Rory was a wolf shifter too? Made sense given that earlier show of canines.

Rory just grunted. "I have merchandise for the right price." He roughly grabbed her arm, yanked her up to stand next to him.

Compared to humans, Nyx was an average height, but next to Rory and the near eight foot tall monster in front of her she felt small. Still, she kept her shoulders straight. She wouldn't cower in front of this male. She wouldn't do that in front of anyone. Ever. That, she knew, was part of her genetic makeup.

"Very pretty merchandise," the male murmured, his pupils going to slits as he looked her over from head to toe. "Where did you get such a lovely fae bitch?"

Rory lifted a shoulder. "None of your fucking business. She's got a mouth—and teeth—on her and I like my females accommodating. I know you don't care so I figured we could do some business. But if you're going to hassle me, I'll find someone else—"

The male shook his head, held up one slightly webbed hand. "I'm interested." He looked at her face, then flicked that creepy gaze to her wings. "I already have a captive to meet my needs, but... she is lovely." His breathing became more rapid. "It's been a while since I've had two females for myself."

"Fuck that!" one of the males nearest the leader said. "You get two prime pieces while we get the leftovers?"

There was grumbling of agreement from a few other males. Dissension in the ranks? Even better, she thought.

The leader's long arm snatched out whip-fast. He wrapped his fingers around the male's neck, squeezed as the male went for a blade strapped to his hip. But the leader was faster. He grabbed his own knife, slammed it through the middle of the subordinate's chest. A thick black liquid oozed from the wound as the male stopped breathing. The leader let him go, then kicked at the male's chest viciously, sending the body flying backward.

"Anyone else want to question me?" he demanded.

No one said a word.

The leader looked back at Rory. "We'll talk business in my tent." His grin grew wide, lecherous as he glanced at Nyx. "You can meet your *other* new bedmate."

"We'll talk right here. I don't want to stay in your filthy camp longer than I have to." Rory's voice was rude, dismissive.

She understood it was because they couldn't go back to the male's tent. It was where his other captive was—where Bo and Ian would be soon if they weren't already.

The leader straightened a fraction, his gaze growing hostile. "Then maybe I just take your whore and kill you."

Rory grinned, the action savage and way more terrifying than she'd ever seen him look. "You could try. But you know my brother's waiting for me and you know what will happen if you try to double cross me." He didn't spell out the threat, but even Nyx could hear the unspoken words hanging in the air. Rory sounded as if he'd raze this whole place to the ground. "Now, can we talk currency exchange or not?"

Gritting his teeth, the leader nodded. "What do you want for her?"

"Dragon bones."

The leader's eyes narrowed even as his pupils turned to vertical slits. The contrasting action was jarring to see. "That's impossible."

Rory lifted a shoulder, casual indifference. "Nothing's impossible. I want them, you want this female. Find me dragon bones, you get her. And she's a virgin."

The male shuddered at that, a huge bulge growing under his loin cloth. Nyx had to swallow back the bile in her throat and force herself not to lash out with her chaos.

It was very, very difficult when every survival instinct told her to kill this male and the surrounding ones who seemed to move closer with each second that ticked by. She wasn't sure if Rory actually knew she was a virgin or if this was just part of his salesman spiel.

Didn't matter because a second later a shrill whistle rent the air. All the males stiffened in alarm, turned at the sound.

Ian and Bo had been discovered.

Rory's talons elongated and he slashed out at the nearest three males, moving lightning fast as he sliced their throats. "Now!" Black ooze flowed down their chests.

But she didn't need his endorsement. She'd already let the leash on her chaos free, shoving out all her energy in a pulsing wave of terror. The surrounding walls didn't crumble, they exploded like geysers.

She ignored the cries and shouts of fear as all the males withdrew their blades and raced toward the nearest opening, away from the falling rubble. They thought they were under attack from an outside force and didn't think twice about dismissing her, of turning their backs to her as if she was a non-threat. She was just a silly fae female they didn't fear.

Their mistake.

While her chaos reigned and the males scrambled to find their unseen oppressors, Rory used the distraction. He threw her over his shoulder and ran. She focused the rest of her energy on the leader even though it wasn't part of their original plan. No matter what happened here today, this male was going to die.

Looking up, she made eye contact with him as Rory flew toward the woods. She mouthed the word "die" seconds before his head exploded.

CHAPTER ELEVEN

Ten minutes earlier

Bo was humming with a raw energy he could barely contain as he and Ian moved into place behind a giant pile of rocks. He'd already shifted to a larger form, his beast growing a few inches in every direction. It only happened to his kind in extreme times of distress and he had no control over it. The single other time it had happened had been when he'd been running Nyx to safety after the collapse of those ruins.

He hadn't even been sure it was a real thing, but now he knew for certain. Ian hadn't shifted though so Bo knew this was directly related to his feelings for Nyx.

Fucking feelings.

They were going to get him killed. He hated that he barely knew how to handle all these emotions. Before her fucking and fighting had been his ways of releasing aggression. And aggression, thanks to his demon half, had been the real emotion he struggled with. This... possessiveness of Nyx was frustrating.

A couple months ago he'd have never thought he could experience such a protectiveness for another be-

144 | KATIE REUS

ing. He loved and felt protective of his sister. But what he felt for Nyx eclipsed that.

And it was at odds with who he was. It sort of went with being a half-demon that caring so deeply for something made you weak. That had been ingrained into him from birth, part of his genetic makeup. Now, the only thing he knew was that if someone tried to take her from him, he'd kill them.

Slowly. Painfully.

"You in control?" Ian murmured, peering around the rocks.

A low grade murmur of male voices had gone up in volume, then quieted. Bo pushed up to see all the males from the back of the camp moving at a fast clip through a set of crumbling pillars. He couldn't see farther without standing on the rocks but he knew Rory had to have breached the place with Nyx in tow. No wonder they were all running, everyone wanted to see her.

Bo rolled his shoulders once, nodded. "Fine."

"There's at least one guard inside the leader's tent. He just went in. We free the females in cages, then move to the tent, take him out. It has to be seamless."

Yeah it did. Nyx's safety depended on it. "I'll take the cage on the left."

Ian nodded and they moved into action, using their stealth and speed to sprint across the open grassy incline to the two huge suspended cages. Bo didn't look at Ian, just focused on his task. He had to trust that his half-brother would do his part. That was another thing he grappled with, trusting these two virtual strangers. His instinct told him he could though. He was betting not only his life on it, but Nyx's.

The bars were strong, but it only took two pulls for him to wrench the door free. The lock snapped off with a clinking sound, the heavy thing slamming to the ground. He froze, looked around but all the males were still about a football field length away with their backs to him and Ian.

The naked female inside with matted black hair was too thin. The outline of her ribs were visible and he wasn't even sure if she was breathing. When he gently reached for her, her eyes flew open. She instantly cringed back from him. Blood and other fluids covered her and it was clear her arm was broken. He couldn't tell what she was exactly. Definitely at least part human, but she could have a mixed heritage.

Didn't matter. "We're here to help you." He reached out a hand for her.

She just closed her eyes, rolled away.

Fuck. He didn't want to jostle her but there was no choice. He just hoped she didn't cry out. Grasping her uninjured upper arm, he pulled her from the cage and into his arms. She stared up at him, but he could tell she wasn't really seeing him.

A burst of rage fired through him. This female had been abused in ways he didn't want to think about. And for a long time. He clamped his jaw shut, shoving back the primal roar he wanted to let loose and looked over at Ian who'd pulled the other female from the cage.

"She's dead," he murmured, his expression as dark as Bo felt. "I still can't leave her here."

Bo nodded once, understanding. No one deserved to be left here. "If we don't kill everyone today I'm coming back." Right now getting Nyx and any survivors to safety was the most important thing but if there were any survivors Bo would come back.

"I'm right there with you." Ian's voice was savage.

Maybe his half-brothers were all right after all. He nodded once in the direction of the biggest tent. It was in the middle of six smaller ones spread out into a half circle. According to Rory it was where another captive was being held.

Bo held the female close to his chest, silently praying for Nyx's safety as they hurried across the open encampment. He was pretty certain no one would listen to his prayers but at this point, he'd try anything.

A move like this was ballsy, but also so damn unexpected that it might work. No, it *would* work.

He refused to accept anything less.

Ian set the dead female down outside the tent door so Bo did the same with the other female. Wincing, she sat up and drew her legs to her chest. He gave her his blade in case she needed to defend herself. He wasn't certain she could even do that but he needed to give her a weapon, give her hope. Moving quickly he stripped off his tunic as well, handed it to her.

He held a finger to his lips before turning to Ian. They'd have one chance to disable the guard before he made a distress call to the others. That was if he was even alone.

Bo counted down from three with his fingers and they rushed in. The doors flapped open.

Two males were standing over a table looking at something. A female was in the corner curled up on a cot. She sat up when she saw them, her eyes wide as she held a blanket up to her neck.

He dismissed her for now and rushed at the males without letting loose the instinctive battle cry building in his throat.

One grabbed a horn from the table, blew into it. Bo slammed into him, cutting off the shrill warning sound as he tackled the male to the ground.

"I'll gut you!" the male shouted, slicing out at Bo with sharp talons similar to his own.

He ignored the threat, ignored everything as he slashed at the male's throat, cutting deep enough to take his head halfway off. Why bother with threats when he could just kill the guy? Out of the corner of his eye he saw Ian disembowel the other Koighan with a grunt of satisfaction, before ripping his head off.

The ground was rumbling and fearful cries filled the air from outside. That meant Nyx was alive to create her chaos. It was the only thing keeping Bo sane right now when he wanted nothing more than to be out there protecting her.

"We're here to help you," Ian said holding his hands up in a calming gesture. It probably didn't help that his hands were covered in blood and other gore. The Irish lilt to his voice was a little thicker as he moved toward the female. Definitely human.

She shoved her blanket off to reveal she was mostly naked except for loose, sheer harem pants. Her blonde hair was pulled back into a braid and she was cleaner and in better shape than the other females but her dark eyes held fear. Her gaze darted to the tent opening then back to them.

"You can leave on your own, we won't stop you, but the Koighans are out there. And we're leaving this realm tonight." He motioned to Bo. "Come with us if you want a chance to live."

He could see the indecision on her face, but after a long moment, she nodded.

"If I carry you we'll go faster," Ian said again.

Bo tamped down his impatience, that growing need to rush out of here and find Nyx. It was easy to hear that the place was falling apart outside.

The female nodded and Ian picked her up as if she weighed nothing.

"I'll carry you like this until we reach the woods. I need an arm free to fight," he explained gently as he slung her over his shoulder.

"I'm going out first," Bo murmured. He needed to re-trieve the other female and though he hated the thought of leaving the dead woman here they would simply have to come back to bury her later. He couldn't carry them both and fight his way out.

He slashed the tent door completely off with his talons in case someone was waiting to attack. His gut twisted at the sight in front of him. The female he'd taken from the cage had stabbed his blade straight through her heart. Without testing her pulse he already knew she was dead.

Ian touched his arm. "We'll come back for them later."

"Take her to the woods. I'll meet you at our rendezvous point."

Ian's jaw clenched, clear he wanted to argue, but Bo wasn't going with them. Ian would be escaping with the female through the back of the encampment and circling back using the woods as cover. It was the securest escape route since there were no Koighans in the way. Bo couldn't do safe now, however.

Not when he had to make sure Nyx was alive. She was his to protect, no matter what. He would prove to her and himself that he was worthy of mating her.

"Go." Then Ian was gone, a flash of movement sprinting toward one of the fallen walls.

Ignoring the twinge of regret in his chest, Bo pulled the blade free from the dead woman and raced toward the front of the ruins. He dodged a falling boulder, jumping into a smoldering fire pit to avoid it. The coals burned his feet but he ignored the pain, ignored everything as he raced through the fray of running Koighans.

Their leader was a mess of blood and body parts and they were all running around like buzzing bees. Typical of their kind. Without someone to lead them and without a visible enemy to fight they revealed their true cowardly nature.

With his left hand he slashed out at the nearest enemy, cut his throat. With his right, he used his blade to slice and dice anything in his way.

Wrong or right, the killing of these monsters let out his aggression in a much needed way.

Up ahead he saw the shimmering flash of Nyx's wings before they disappeared into the line of trees. His relief was short lived as he saw the yellow flash of a Koighan fleeing into the woods. Maybe the male wasn't going after Nyx, but it didn't matter.

The male was dead.

On a burst of speed, Bo gave into his savagery, gave into everything that made him a half-demon. He let the darkest part of himself take over until he was barely in control.

It seemed as if only a second had passed from the time he exited the ruins to when he flew through the line of trees.

The male was ahead, racing full speed. A blade was in his hand.

Bo could see the shimmer of Nyx's wings through the thick foliage. The other male had to see it too. She was like a beacon to anything and everything in this realm.

And they were about out of time before darkness fell. The sun wouldn't set like it did on earth. It would be an abrupt change from light to darkness.

Closer, closer, the male was almost within reach. Bo reared back, threw the knife with all his force. It made a soft singing sound as it flew through the air.

The male started to turn, but it was too late.

Thud.

It embedded in the back of the enemy's neck, right where his head and spine joined. Bo slowed a few paces as he reached the fallen male, yanked out the blade and kept running.

His feet barely touched the ground as he gained speed, jumping over roots and fallen trees. Only when he spotted Nyx standing on her own two feet next to Rory, and Ian and the other female at their rendezvous point, did he allow himself the smallest breath of relief.

Nyx was safe. Alive.

His.

As he reached them he pulled her into his arms, holding her close. He was vaguely aware of the other female making a distressed sound and when he saw her face realized the female thought he was hurting Nyx.

Not in this lifetime. Not in any lifetime. But he forced himself to loosen his grip and pull back. He was covered in the thick blood of some of his victims and other grime, but couldn't find it in him to care. "You're okay?"

She nodded, looking him over as if making sure he was okay. He wasn't used to a female other than family caring about him. It was jarring, but he liked it—craved it from her. Probably too much. "The leader's dead. There weren't any others?"

His lips pulled into a thin line. He'd tell her later. Now he just shook his head.

"We need to go. Now." Rory scooped up the other female in an oddly possessive way, baring his teeth at his very surprised brother before racing off toward the stream they'd come from.

"Come on." Ian fell behind his brother, moving at a fast clip.

"You want me to carry you?" Bo asked Nyx. "We'll go faster."

Thankfully she nodded. Relief slid through him that she was letting him care for her. The need to hold her, protect her, was overwhelming. Instead of tossing her over his shoulder as he'd done before, this time he scooped her up and held her to his chest. She curled into him, laying her head against him in a way that said she trusted him completely.

The action and feel of her so close to him soothed the primal need to destroy he'd felt when she'd headed into that camp without his protection. Now she was safe in his arms, he wasn't letting her go. Soon he'd make her his completely.

"I had no idea half-demons could move this fast," she murmured against his chest.

She sounded almost glad he was a half-demon. Yep, he was going to imprint himself on every inch of her body so that she never forgot the feel of him, the scent of him. He was going to bind her to him in the most primal way so that she'd never want to leave.

* * *

"I don't mind going in first," Nyx said, frowning at Bo as he tried to completely bar the entrance to the small opening of the cave.

He just snorted and crouched down before managing to squeeze his big body through the opening.

Their group was on the side of a small mountain and they had about ten minutes before it was dark. Since it would take about an hour to reach the realm exit—and according to Ian and Rory would be difficult to find at night—they'd decided to find shelter for the evening. She just hoped this cave worked because right now they all needed to recharge. Rory said he'd been in it before and it didn't have another exit, but Bo wanted to check it out before they all entered. She knew Bo could take care of himself, but she still wanted him to get some rest. After the day they'd had, he needed it and she knew he'd never admit it. The male was too stubborn.

Less than a minute later he called out. "It's empty."

Rory nodded at Nyx and the other female who still hadn't spoken. They'd given her a tunic, which swallowed her, but she didn't seem to mind. Nyx didn't want to think about what she'd been through.

"You two go first. We've got your back," Rory said.

Nyx motioned to the female. "You can go first."
When she hesitated Nyx asked, "You want me to go instead?" The female nodded, relief in her dark eyes.

She couldn't exactly blame the female for not wanting to enter a cave with a male she didn't know. Bo was big and scary and even though Ian and Rory were too, Rory seemed to have taken up the role of the female's protector.

The opening was small and close to the ground, but she slid through easy enough. The light from Bo's eyes lit up the small enclosure. There wasn't much to it. The cave was about two feet higher than Bo and wide enough that they could all rest for a few hours. Any longer though, and the place would get cramped.

A chill raked over her skin, making her shiver. Bo was at her side and had his arm wrapped around her shoulders before she could blink. She leaned into him, not caring about anything that had happened between them over the last couple of days. At least not at the moment. She just wanted to get everyone in here and hope they were safe until morning. Survival trumped everything at the moment.

And Bo made her feel safe. Curling up with him and crashing sounded like the best idea she'd ever had. She just hoped the male had finally pulled his head out of his ass.

When everyone was inside, Ian and Bo simultaneously moved to a pile of rocks as if they'd choreographed

the movement and shifted some to the opening, blocking it off.

"I'll stay up for first watch," Ian said, turning to everyone.

The only light in the cave was from the brothers'
eyes. The combined multicolored glow was dim, but
enough that she could clearly see everyone.

"I'll take the second," Bo said.

Rory nodded at him. "I'll take the last. We can break
it up so that we each take only three and a half hour
shifts."

Nyx thought that maybe she should be offended that
they weren't including her in the shifts but she really
didn't care because it meant she'd get more sleep. The
thought made her feel bad though. "I can easily take a
shift—"

"No," the three said, practically simultaneously.

"Is this like a sexist thing?" She'd never really dealt
with sexism until entering the human realm. In her
mother's realm and even with her father's people, power
was all that mattered. Gender didn't come into the equa-
tion.

Ian lifted a shoulder. "Maybe, I don't know. Don't
care either. You're not taking a shift."

She blinked at his authoritative tone and glanced at
Bo who simply nodded in agreement. "He's right. You
need rest. So does she." He tilted his chin at the female
who'd basically collapsed against the hard ground in a
sitting position. "And we all need to eat."

Since it wasn't worth arguing over, Nyx nodded and moved to one of the backpacks as the males did the same with theirs. She snorted as she pulled out a plastic jar. The brothers had packed supplies for everyone, but she hadn't seen what they'd included until now. "Peanut butter? And... beef jerky?"

"I gave you teriyaki flavor," Rory said without looking at her as he moved quietly and quickly to sit directly next to the female.

"Did you steal this from that chef guy too?" she asked.

Ian's wicked grin was answer enough.

The food seemed a little weird but it would give them energy and calories. Nyx watched as Rory awkwardly held out his jar of peanut butter and a canteen of water to the female. Nyx wanted to ask her so many questions; like what her name was, who the other women had been, where she was from, how long she'd been stuck here. But none of that mattered and it was clear the female didn't want to speak. Nyx certainly wasn't going to push her. She was, however, going to make sure she got medical attention once they got back to the human realm. Ophelia, the Stavros pack healer, would see the female immediately, Nyx had no doubt. Or Victoria too, if she was still in Biloxi.

"You want mine?" Bo handed her his bag of sweet 'n spicy jerky.

She grinned, took his bag. "Thanks. You want mine?"

Nodding in relief, he took hers and sidled up next to her. She noticed Ian had moved and was eating by the rocked-off exit, quietly watching Rory with what looked like... concern. She wasn't sure though. And she wasn't going to worry about it.

As she chewed the jerky, she laid her head against Bo's shoulder. She liked touching him. It grounded her. "I'm glad you're okay," she murmured. Clearly the male could take care of himself, but that hadn't stopped her from worrying about him. She didn't think anything could do that.

"Right back at you." A shudder seemed to go through him. "It was difficult to let you go. And I'm not questioning your ability to protect yourself," he tacked on quickly. "Especially not after what you did to the Koighan leader."

She looked up at him, half-grinned. That male had deserved the death he'd gotten, had probably deserved worse. "It was grosser than I'd imagined." Seeing him pretty much explode had been, well, there were no words for it. It was like something out of a science fiction movie.

"He's dead?" the female asked, the first words she'd spoken.

Nyx looked over at her, surprised by the soft southern accent. "The leader? Yes."

Tears rolled down her cheeks and she set down her jar of peanut butter. "Good." She turned away from them then and simply laid down on the rocky ground.

Rory whipped off his tunic and rolled it up into a makeshift pillow before sliding it under her head. He looked so confused, as if he didn't know what to do. But there was a simmering anger under the surface she could see clearly in the way his eyes had brightened.

Appetite gone, Nyx closed up her jerky bag. She wished she could leave the cave and finish off the rest of the monsters from that camp. None of them deserved to live. She glanced at Bo. "You want to get some sleep before your shift?"

He simply nodded and stretched out, using the backpack as a pillow before pulling her own backpack close to his. He patted the ground next to him. As if she'd consider sleeping anywhere else. Not after everything they'd been through. For tonight, she would shelve everything and just sleep next to the sexy, sometimes frustrating male. She needed to feel his warmth against her, needed to know he was alive and safe.

"I want you to sleep next to me," he murmured, his voice almost unsure.

Eyelids heavy, she turned around so that her back curved against his stomach and chest. She wasn't surprised when his arm snagged around her and pulled her closer. "I wouldn't sleep anywhere else." A sense of peace rolled over her as his grip tightened. Being with him calmed her in the best way possible. Made her feel safe, wanted, protected.

He'd managed to clean off most of the blood when they'd raced through the stream and change into a clean tunic, but they were all filthy. And she didn't even care.

With the exception of everyone's breathing, the cave was mostly silent. Rory hadn't laid down yet, but seemed to be humming with energy as he hovered near the female. He looked so damn lost. Ian was casually leaning against the wall next to the blocked-off entrance, quietly eating his jerky.

Even though she and Bo didn't have privacy, she didn't care. There was something that had been on her mind and after today, she trusted Ian and Rory to overhear their conversation. "I've been thinking about something," she murmured.

"What?" Bo's grip tightened just a fraction.

"It can't be a coincidence that we ended up in the same realm your half-brothers live in. Technically I guess it could, but... I don't believe in coincidences that huge. What if the person the trap was set for wasn't me?"

Bo's breathing was a steady rise and fall against her back. "I thought about that too." His voice was just as quiet as hers had been. "But I can't imagine why someone would want to send me here to meet my relatives. If anything, if we ended up becoming friends, it just strengthens us. Not sure how that benefits anyone looking to harm me."

"Not even your father?"

He snorted and so did Ian, a reminder she didn't need that the others could hear their conversation. "It's probably a disadvantage to him for us to become friends."

"Hmm, yeah." That made sense. Frowning, she closed her eyes, trying to figure out why whoever had sent them here—and she was leaning toward it being her mother because it was the only thing that made sense with that stupid package delivery—and why. She couldn't imagine why her mother would have sent Nyx here though. Unless she'd just wanted Nyx to suffer or die? That thought... hurt. No matter how much she tried to tell herself she hated her family.

"Does my demon form... disturb you?" Bo asked a few minutes later, his voice so quiet she almost didn't hear him.

The question surprised her, but she didn't have to think about it. "You're the most magnificent, beautiful being I've ever seen," she murmured, her words drowsy. Even the creepy animal cries from outside the cave bare-ly phased her. She was too exhausted to be worried.

"I don't think males are supposed to be beautiful." She could hear the smile in his voice now.

"You are, something I think you already know." She reached back and patted his hip once, ignoring the feel of his erection against her back. Even if it pleased her that he was affected by her.

He covered her hand with his bigger one, slid his fin-gers through hers and tucked their hands in front of her stomach, keeping her close to him.

Sighing, she closed her eyes and forgot about every-thing else except for the way Bo was holding her. What-ever had happened between them before, whatever had scared him away from her, they would work out. She had to believe that.

* * *

Rory couldn't stop the energy humming through him as he stared up at the ceiling of the cave. He'd tried sleeping, but he couldn't do it. Not when he scented the pain rolling off the quiet, nameless female curled up into a ball on the ground a foot away from him. He'd put another tunic over her as a makeshift blanket when she'd finally dozed and hated that he couldn't do more for her.

The scent of her emotions and her unique scent, it was doing something strange to him. As a half-demon, half-shifter, he had naturally heightened senses, but this was different than anything he'd ever experienced.

His wolf was clawing at him, demanding he do something for the female. Something more than a pathetic covering. In this realm he was more in control than the human realm, but even so, his wolf wanted out.

Now.

He wanted to hunt and destroy.

They'd be leaving in the morning and it would be too late then. Now, when the Koighans were weak and without a leader he could destroy them all. Eradicate them completely from this realm. They wouldn't have gone far from their encampment considering the time of day they'd been attacked. Some might still even be there.

Didn't matter. He'd be able to scent them.

Quietly he pushed up and looked around the cave. Bo was keeping watch by the entry and the others were all sleeping.

Moving on silent feet he hurried to his half-brother, crouched down. "I need out."

Bo's eyes flashed brighter, his expression of annoyance so similar to Ian's it took Rory off guard for a moment. "Out of the cave?" The underlying question was "are you crazy?" Maybe he was.

"I need to hunt down the rest of the Koighans. I need to do it for her." He wished he knew what her name was. "She won't be able to move on if..." He couldn't finish the words, could barely talk. It didn't matter that the leader was dead, they all needed to die. His brother had told him what condition those two other females had been in; one even taking her own life instead of being rescued.

Bo was silent as he watched him. Then to Rory's surprise, his half-brother simply nodded and hefted up one of the stones. As soon as he did a rush of fresh air filled the cavern. "We leave at daybreak."

He nodded and stripped, leaving his clothes in a pile inside the cave. For this hunt, he was shifting to his wolf.

As his natural instincts to hunt kicked in, his wolf completely taking over, the only thought he was aware of was that he would avenge his female. Those males would all die for what they'd done.

CHAPTER TWELVE

Even though she wasn't particularly hungry, Nyx scooped out some peanut butter from her jar with a plastic spoon. They'd be leaving soon and she'd need all the energy she could get for the exit. She'd already put her tunic back on, covering her wings. As soon as Rory returned—from wherever he'd disappeared to—they'd be heading out.

"Are you from the human realm, uh, Earth?" Nyx asked the female who was quietly eating beef jerky.

She nodded. Her blonde hair had come slightly loose from the braid during the night and she had dark circles under her eyes.

"That's where we're going soon."

The female's dark eyes lit up with something that looked a lot like hope before she quickly masked it. She just tore into the dried meat and kept chewing.

Nyx wished there was something she could do to alleviate the woman's suffering. She was a demigod but absolutely useless. "I'm Nyx, by the way. I know we weren't technically introduced."

No response, but the female nodded and gave her a half-smile as she continued eating.

Bo and Ian were in the corner near the entrance talking in tones so low she couldn't hear them, but it was clear Ian was annoyed. Maybe about where Rory had gone?

When one of the heavy stones blocking the entrance starting moving inward, both Ian and Bo tensed, their talons sliding out as they faced off with the intruder.

Nyx started to channel her energy when Rory's muffled voice filtered through the opening. "Some help with this thing?"

The two males tugged it toward them, letting Rory in. Daylight trickled inside. A burst of hope bloomed inside Nyx. They'd be going home soon. Even if she didn't technically have a home, they wouldn't be in this hell anymore. Sure she was staying at Bo's, but... she wasn't even sure what was going on with them at this point.

Rory crawled through and stood—completely naked, covered in healing nicks and bruises and a little blood. She didn't think it was his though. He nodded at the female, his expression fierce. "All the Koighans are dead. Every single one."

The woman didn't respond as Rory dressed, but surprise and relief flickered in her dark gaze.

Nyx stood, picked up her backpack, but Bo was faster, plucking it from her. "Hopefully we won't need these pretty soon."

"No kidding."

Moving slowly, Bo reached out and cupped her cheek. He gently rubbed his thumb against her skin, his gaze unreadable. The effect of him touching her, even in this hell, was potent. He didn't say anything, just gave her an intense look that said he wanted to strip her naked and do wicked, wicked things to her, before he turned to face his brothers. "Let's get the fuck out of here."

She swallowed hard, trying to keep focused but it was hard when her thoughts were all over the place thanks to Bo. Nyx wondered if the other two males were coming with them through the exit. They'd never actually said, but from the way they'd been acting since leaving that camp, she thought they might be. Especially considering the possessive looks Rory had been giving the rescued female.

By the time they'd trekked to the exit point, slower this morning, since they had a human with them and she'd walked part of the way, it had taken two hours.

But they were here, on the outskirts of the forest in front of a lagoon.

Nyx wanted to do freaking cartwheels.

"So where's the exit?" Nyx asked, looking out at the crystal clear lavender lagoon from the shoreline.

The whole place was too peaceful. Too... weird. The lagoon area was surrounded by a high, sharp-faced mountainside to the west and a jungle on the other side of it. But there wasn't much noise and no wind. The shoreline was rocky instead of sandy.

"It's at the bottom of the pool. We'll have to swim hard to reach it," Rory murmured, dropping his backpack. "Leave everything unless you absolutely need it. We can't have anything weighing us down. Once the door opens, it'll suck us in fast."

"I can't swim," the blonde rasped out, raw terror in her voice as she stared at them.

It took Nyx a moment to realize the woman thought they would leave her behind.

Before she could reassure her that they wouldn't, Bo said, "We're not going to leave you behind." The way he said it was matter-of-fact.

"You can hold onto my back," Rory said, almost simultaneously while Ian simply nodded. "Will you be able to hold your breath?"

The female nodded.

"Any creatures we need to be aware of lurking in the water?" Bo asked, stripping off his tunic.

Nyx forced herself not to stare at the ripped lines and ridges of his muscular chest and abs. Definitely not appropriate timing. Still... her gaze trailed down, down, down, to the band of his pants before she felt herself flushing. Oh yeah, no matter what happened when they got back, she was going to take all he had to offer. No doubt about it.

"Nope. Not that we know of anyway." Rory glanced out at the still water. "But the swim is strenuous, and the matter of finding the exit can be difficult. We've done it multiple times though. The only problem is... it doesn't always spit you out in the same place every time."

"So we could end up in freaking Antarctica?" Nyx asked, taking her tunic off. It was too heavy to swim in. Her flimsy top beneath it was dingy but it would have to do.

"Pretty much." His voice was wry.

That sucked, but it was still okay. She'd be able to transport them wherever they wanted to go once they were in the human realm. Once they were free.

Nyx noticed that the blonde wasn't taking off her tunic. The material was thick, way too heavy for a hard swim. Nyx looked at the three males. "Turn around."

To her surprise they all faced the water. She stripped off her top and handed it to the female. "Wear this instead." Nyx had a bra on and didn't relish the thought of wearing only it in front of everyone but this woman deserved to get back a sense of control over her life.

"You're sure?" she spoke, surprising Nyx.

She nodded. "Yeah. That tunic is way too heavy for the water. Oh, hold on..." She dug her ripped jeans out of the backpack and went to stand in front of Bo while the woman changed into her top. "Will you cut these into shorts with your talons?" It would take him seconds.

He growled at the sight of her in just her bra, but she pressed a finger to his lips. He nipped at her finger, taking her off guard. Heat pooled low in her belly as he gently bit the tip, then sucked the finger into his mouth.

168 | KATIE REUS

"Bo," she murmured. Now was so not the time.

He let out a frustrated grumble but took the jeans and made quick work of them.

"They might be a little loose," Nyx said as she handed them to the blonde.

"I don't care. Thank you." The woman stepped into them and sure enough they were a little too big, but they would do for the trip.

Unfortunately Nyx was going to have to strip her harem-style pants off for the swim too because there was no way she could swim with them slowing her pace. Bo would just have to deal with her lack of clothing.

Once they were all ready to go, the males naked, the blonde in ripped, dirty clothing and Nyx in her bra and underwear, she inwardly cringed at the sight they made. If they ended up in a populated area when they exited this realm, some strangers were in for an eyeful.

"We're going to swim out to the middle of the lagoon," Rory said, stepping close to the blonde. "The dive down is about three hundred feet."

"The longest free dive is something like seven hundred feet," Nyx said. And that was for trained professionals. She wasn't worried about dying, but she didn't know if the human could hold her breath that long.

Bo lifted an eyebrow. "How do you even know that?"

"Victoria told me."

"Ah." He nodded, apparently having received all the explanation he needed. Victoria was the queen of dropping random, obscure facts for absolutely no reason. It was one of the things Nyx adored about the female.

"Yes, so it's far," Rory continued. "We'll have to stay close together because like I said, once the door opens it'll pull us in fast. No one wants to get left behind. If you miss this opening, it'll take another entire day to open again. It's triggered by our bodies."

Nyx wanted to ask what would happen if someone had already used it this morning, but kept quiet. She figured they'd already thought of that. And if someone had recently opened it, then they'd just have to try again tomorrow. Unfortunately she didn't think the blonde female could hold her breath long enough for the return trip up if it ended up being necessary. Worried, Nyx started to say something when the blonde shook her head.

"I'll risk it," she said, clearly having the same thought as Nyx. "I'm not staying here another night. If I die, I'm dying free."

Okay then. As they waded into the crisp, cool water, Bo gently touched her arm. "I'm a strong swimmer."

Not to mention he would have much longer strokes. "Do you want me on your back?"

He nodded and she realized he was trying to give her the option, not order her.

"Once we reach the middle of the lagoon I will. Thank you," she murmured. She didn't want to slow the group down, not when they'd only get one chance at this.

Perched on his back, the blonde hooked her arms around Rory's neck as soon as it got deep enough, but Nyx swam through the cool, still water until Rory and Ian stopped.

Nyx moved behind Bo, sliding her arms and legs around him as he treaded water. He hadn't been kidding, he was a very strong swimmer. He didn't seem the least bit winded from their swim and she guessed it to be about fifty yards. She knew she shouldn't have been paying attention to him, but her surroundings instead. But seeing the way his body cut through the water with such fluid precision was breathtaking and hard to ignore.

"I'm going to miss seeing you in this form," she murmured close to his ear as she pressed her mostly naked body against his bare back.

He jerked slightly, sending out a ripple in the water.

"Ready?" Ian asked, looking at them.

Nyx nodded as Bo said, "Yes."

She took a deep breath right before they went under the surface. Burying her face against the back of his neck she held on tight as he went deeper and deeper. Her lungs started to burn after a while.

She opened her eyes and even though the water was clear it had gotten much darker. The urge to draw in a breath was becoming more and more urgent but she knew they'd be there soon. Or she really hoped they would—

A flash of light nearly blinded her as the water parted all around them, throwing them into the vortex. She sucked in a burst of air as water whipped around them like a cocoon, but didn't touch them any longer. They were spinning out of control, a kaleidoscope of colors bursting from every direction, bathing them in a rainbow of sensations.

"Ugh," she grunted as her back came in contact with something solid. She found herself looking up at a sky filled with a billion stars. At least the transport had dried her. Groaning, she shoved up to see the others doing the same thing.

Bo was lying next to her, looking slightly dazed as he moved to a sitting position. They were in a grassy field with no discernable man-made lights and it was pretty cold.

"Anyone know where we are?" Rory asked and she got her first good look at both him and his brother in human form.

They looked similar, both white, unlike Bo, but like Bo they were pretty big all over. And they had espresso-colored hair. "I didn't picture you with a beard," she said, eyeing Rory. The truth was, she hadn't really pictured them at all.

He just laughed before looking over at the woman, concern in his eyes. She was sitting up, looking around in wonder.

"You've got to tell us your name," Nyx said, taking the hand Bo extended to her to pull her to her feet. The air was crisp and fresh with a hint of... manure? Gah, they must be in some sort of animal pasture if the baying sounds nearby were any indication.

"Liberty," she murmured, wiping her hands off against her cut-off shorts.

"It shouldn't be too hard to find transportation, but first we've gotta find clothes," Ian said, looking around the wide open field.

Nyx purposefully avoided looking at everyone's junk. Besides Bo, she was tired of seeing all these naked body parts. "That won't be a problem. I can just transport us to Bo's place." She glanced at him then, eyebrows raised. "Unless—"

"My house is perfect."

That meant he trusted his brothers, something that made her inordinately happy. She trusted them too.

"Uh, transport?" Ian asked, running a hand through his close-cropped, dark hair.

"Yeah. You all just need to touch me. My arms or wherever. Then we can go." She looked at Liberty. "And if you want to go somewhere else, I'll take you wherever you want once we've gotten back to Biloxi."

"You're from Biloxi?" Her eyes widened slightly.

"I live there." For now.

"I'm from... I know the city."

When it was clear she didn't plan to say more, Nyx looked at everyone. "Unless you guys like the smell of cow poop, I'm ready to go." And to get into some real clothes.

Bo moved behind her, holding onto her hips in a very possessive way while the others just touched her forearms. She loved the feel of him holding her like this, wanted to sink into it.

"Hold on," she murmured, focusing on a memory of Bo's kitchen. It was big enough to hold all of them and she already knew Bo could put everything she broke back together.

When they landed in his kitchen she was surprised that only a few of the glass front cabinets shattered. Thankfully he put them back together before any of the shards blasted over them.

"What are you people?" Liberty asked, eyes wide as she wrapped her arms around herself as she leaned against the center island.

Bo cleared his throat and looked at his brothers. "Half-demon, half-human," he said. He knew what Rory was, but he hadn't figured out what Ian was yet. Some sort of shifter for certain though.

"Half-demon, half-wolf shifter," Rory said.

"Half-demon too," Ian said, evading answering what else he was.

Bo wasn't going to push though. Because they had too many damn things to take care of first. And he didn't want Nyx to answer. It didn't appear that she planned to but still, he said, "Everyone needs clothes, and Liberty, I think maybe..." He looked at Nyx for help. It was clear the human had been abused but he didn't want to overwhelm her with too much at once.

"Oh, um, we're friends with a wolf pack in this territory and they have a healer. If you'd like to talk to her before calling your family or..." Nyx looked just as lost as he felt.

The female cleared her throat. "Is a healer like a doctor, I'm assuming?"

Nyx nodded. "Yes."

"I'd like to talk to her and I don't really have any family." She looked so damn lost and broken, the exhaustion on her face more prominent now. The grip she had around herself was tight and though it was subtle, she was trembling.

"You have us," Rory blurted, then flushed, looking incredibly uncomfortable when Liberty gave him a surprised look.

"You can stay here as long as you'd like," Bo said, something urging him to make the offer. He valued his privacy and space, but this woman needed the shelter. When Nyx looked over at him as if he'd just hung the moon, well, yeah, it felt fucking good.

"Really?" Liberty asked.

"Yeah, you all can," he added, looking at his brothers. They still had a lot to discuss but for now, they could all rest.

And he needed to call his sister and he knew Nyx would want to contact Finn and the Stavros pack regardless of calling their healer. Once all that was figured out, he and Nyx were talking.

More than talking. She was his. He was going to just lay it all on the line, tell her what he wanted. He needed to man up and do it. He just hoped she'd still have him.

* * *

"Thurman seems okay," Drake said, glancing around the small café with the eyes of a predator.

After spending over a thousand years in Hell he viewed every situation as a potential threat. Most shifters tended to size up rooms and people as a general rule, but Victoria's mate was vigilant in a way she only saw in certain types of shifters. Alphas. And hers was one to the bone. "I'm glad you think so. He really is a kind man." It was clear Thurman felt guilt over the theft of the spell. Not that he could have prevented it, not against someone powerful enough to erase his memories.

"He should be here by now though." Drake frowned, leaned back in the chair that was a little too small for his huge frame as he glanced out the open window next to their table.

Live music from a band playing on the sidewalk a block down filtered in from outside, mixing with the soft jazz music of the restaurant. The city was loud and boisterous and tonight was no different.

"He's only five minutes late. That means nothing." Especially not in the South. Something Drake knew by now. People took their sweet time.

He just grunted, linked his fingers through hers and practically growled at the approaching waitress. Which was definitely not like him. Normally he was all politeness mixed with awkwardness.

"Two café au laits," Victoria said to her with a smile. "All right, what's going on?" she murmured to her mate once they were alone again. Well, alone as they'd ever be in a restaurant packed to capacity.

"I don't like these seats." He looked out the long, floor to ceiling windows right next to their table.

A couple with a bulldog wearing a pink sweater strolled past, caught up in their conversation. She knew he didn't care about their actual seating, just that they weren't in the best tactical position. Sitting in a restaurant right off Chartres Street, they were at a table with wide open windows with easy access for anyone to attack. When people walked by, all Victoria and Drake would have to do was reach out a hand and they'd be able to touch them. "I can call Thurman and tell him we'll meet him somewhere else." Because if her mate was feeling edgy, she didn't want to ignore that instinct.

"No." He pushed out a breath, giving her one of those sheepish smiles that made her belly flip-flop. "It's just... been over a year since I got out."

Of Hell, he meant. She swallowed hard at the mention, hated that he'd lost so many years of his very long life in the worst place imaginable. And yet he'd somehow retained his goodness. She squeezed his hand, cupped his cheek. "Do you want to leave?"

"No, no, I just meant, I don't know. Some days I think I'll wake up and find out this is a dream. That you're a dream."

Her throat tightened as she looked into the stormy gray eyes of her mate. Victoria was vaguely aware of their server leaving their drinks, thankfully not interrupting as she left them alone. "It's not a dream, baby. You know how you should know?"

His jaw clenched tight as he shook his head once.

"Because you never, *ever* would have been able to dream up someone as awesome as me," she whispered, somehow keeping her tone serious.

Just like she intended, he laughed, one of those deep, real laughs he rarely gave her or anyone else. His beautiful smile blinded her as he shook his head, his shoulders trembling with laughter. "I love you so much," he murmured, kissing her forehead, then her mouth in a light brush she felt all the way to her toes.

She started to lean into it, not caring about their surroundings, when he stiffened ever so slightly and pulled back. She turned around, following his gaze to see Thurman and a male, who was definitely a vampire, striding their way. Supernaturals moved with a sort of inherent stealth, their movements more economic than humans.

She and Drake automatically stood as a unified front when Thurman and the vampire reached their table.

"Apologies for being late. Parking's a nightmare today," Thurman said with a polite nod of his head. He still wore the three piece suit. She loved how put together the man always seemed to be.

Drake shook his head, as if it didn't bother him at all. "It's no problem."

"Shall we sit?" she asked, motioning to the four chairs.

"Yes, thank you. Victoria, Drake, this is Abraham."

The blond-haired, blue-eyed vampire with pale skin looked like an unassuming college student. She sensed some of his power, but if she had to guess, he was young, probably turned in the last fifty years. The male clearly sensed Drake's power, not that her mate was blocking it very well, because he gave them both a nervous smile, his gaze lingering on Drake with just a touch of fear. Which didn't bother Victoria at all. She wanted this vampire to be truthful with them and it was more likely he would be if he was afraid.

"Pleased to meet you," she murmured. "Thank you for agreeing to speak with us."

He nodded once. "I'm not sure what I can tell you, but I want to help."

She didn't scent that typical acidic smell associated with a lie coming off him, but only time would tell if he was being truthful.

"Do you remember anything from the night Thurman's shop was robbed?" Drake asked point blank.

The vampire looked at Thurman before focusing on the two of them again. "No. But I've been having...

dreams the past few days. As if memories are trying to surface, but I don't trust them. The memories."

Victoria straightened in her seat. "What do you mean?"

"I don't know how to explain it. I know someone messed with my mind." His jaw tightened, his eyes going bright for a moment before he closed them, getting himself under control.

Yep, he had to be young.

They all paused as the server returned to take the others' drink orders. To be polite Victoria ordered a couple appetizers for the table but she wasn't certain they'd make it that far. She and Drake just wanted answers so they could head home. They'd had to wait for nightfall and then for Thurman to retrieve his vampire friend.

"Like I was saying," Abraham continued. "I know my memory was erased but I also think fake ones were input as well."

Victoria frowned. That was possible, though again very, *very* hard to do. With a supernatural being, there was no guarantee that the fake memories or even the memory loss would stick. It would have been easier to simply kill Thurman and Abraham. Which she also found interesting. It seemed as if the being behind the theft wasn't a total monster.

"Why do you say that?" Drake asked.

"I… have no idea. Instinct."

"What are you remembering in your dreams?"

"An old woman, probably in her nineties, at the shop, asking about wormhole packages." He rubbed a hand over his face, shaking his head once. "I get these flashes of her face. She looks human, but…" He pushed out a breath, his frustration clear. "More than the memories, I just sense power. A lot of it. That, I'm pretty sure is real. And that's all I can tell you. Other than I'm pissed about this whole thing."

It didn't tell them much, but Victoria nodded. Even if she only had a small theory right about now. "Will you contact us if you remember more?" she asked, looking between Thurman and Abraham.

They both nodded and murmured acquiescence, then Drake's phone buzzed. His eyebrows raised as he looked at the screen. "Bo's home," he murmured.

Relief surged through Victoria, but she simply nodded. It was definitely time to leave. She turned to Thurman as Drake pulled out a few bills. "I apologize for leaving so abruptly but the people that… package was used on, are back. We need to go."

Thurman's head tilted to the side a fraction as he looked between them. "Are you referring to Bo Broussard?"

"Ah, yes," Victoria answered. She couldn't imagine why it would hurt for Thurman or the vamp to know. "You know him?"

His mouth curved up. "Haven't seen him in a few decades. He's from here, you know."

"I do know."

"I was a little in love with his mother. So many of us were," he murmured, his eyes clouding over for a moment before he seemed to gather himself. "He's okay then?"

"I hope so. I'll let you know."

"Please do."

"If you need any help here with anything else, call me," she said, meaning it. "This shouldn't have happened to you. My pack will help if you need anything." The man was like an institution in New Orleans. He was well liked and respected by both humans and supernaturals. What had happened to him was just wrong.

"Thank you."

After murmuring a polite goodbye, Drake linked his fingers through hers and they made their way out into the loud, colorful streets of New Orleans. At least her mate was less tense now. She had questions, but she'd wait until they were alone. Their next stop would be somewhere private so her mate could shift and they could fly back to Biloxi.

CHAPTER THIRTEEN

"Ophelia is a good female," Bo said, leaning against the wall outside one of his guest bedrooms, watching Rory pace up and down the hallway like a madman. "And Nyx is in there. The female is fine." As fine as she could be given the circumstances.

"I'm not worried," Rory muttered, looking at him as if he was insane.

Bo just snorted. "Right." Ian had gone downstairs, supposedly in search of food, but Bo guessed it was because of his brother's incessant pacing. Finn was down there with him, probably questioning him about how long he planned to be in his territory, since he was half shifter. "So, you're Scottish?" The accent was a dead giveaway even if he hadn't already told him where he was from, but Bo needed the male to stop moving. Even if that meant small talk. Rory was giving him a headache.

"Yeah."

"What pack were you part of?"

Rory ran a hand over his hair, his green eyes flashing in annoyance. "Are you trying to distract me?"

Bo lifted a shoulder. "Maybe. I'm also curious about my... brother." It felt weird, but good to say it.

Rory gave him a half-smile. "My mother was a beta wolf. It was how a demon... well, you know." His expression darkened at that. "Anyway, I haven't seen her pack in almost a hundred years. When she died I split. They always treated me *differently* so I'm sure they didn't miss me." The bitterness in that word said they treated him more than just different.

Bo nodded. Half-demons were often looked upon like the plague of the supernatural world. Things had changed in the last decade or so, but yeah, he understood. Nyx had never looked at him any differently though. Something that stunned him. Still, he felt that deep-seated urge to prove himself. To prove that he wasn't like his father. "You ever join another pack?"

"I tried. Didn't take. Then I met Ian."

Bo nodded again. "How long has it been since you've been in the human realm?"

"'Bout a year, give or take. We spend most of our time in one of the Hell realms, but we..." He scrubbed a hand over the back of his neck. "We have money, investments, land, mostly in the States. Some in our homeland, Europe. We check on them once or twice every year, make sure we're still getting richer, then head back to our realm. We're not going to mooch off you if that's what you're worried about."

"I wasn't worried." He hadn't even thought of that possibility when normally that would have been his first assumption. Unlike Nyx, who seemed to look for the good in people, he normally saw the bad. It was simply what he expected based on experience and his cynical nature. This last year, however, he'd had some of his perceptions changed. A freaking wolf shifter had recently mated with a vampire and they'd been housing a dragon shifter—more than one—just because they could. In his experience people, regardless of species, tended to be assholes.

"Oh... well, good. We can get a place tomorrow if you'd rather have your space."

Bo shook his head, frowning. He wanted space for him and Nyx but his place was huge and had incredible insulation. He'd just found his brothers and while he didn't want them to stay indefinitely, a few days or weeks was fine. "Look, I don't want fucking roommates, but... a few weeks is cool. Besides, you really gonna leave *her*?" He tilted his head to the closed door.

Rory just frowned and resumed his pacing.

"We have a sister." Bo had already talked to her and she'd be there soon. Better to tell them first.

Rory turned back to Bo, blinked once. "Seriously?"

"Yeah, she's a half-vamp."

"Our father just assaulted every species didn't he." Not a question, but a statement of truth, his words laced with disgust. Rory turned away, started the pacing again.

"Cynara—that's her name. Her mom had just been turned when she was raped. She was still weak, not quite human, not quite vampire." Because the only other option for a vampire to have a child was to have a bloodborn. And those were very rare. Not to mention way too powerful for someone to overpower, even a demon.

"We should find more of our siblings and end that fucker," Rory said, more to himself it seemed.

But Bo agreed, had had the same thought more than once. He just didn't think he could go up against his father on his own. And until recently he'd never trusted anyone enough to ask them to go after the bastard. Doing so would most likely mean loss of life so whoever joined him would have to be committed and have a reason to want the guy dead.

Before he could respond, the door to Liberty's room opened and Ophelia and Nyx walked out. Nyx immediately moved to Bo, her expression unreadable. She hovered next to him instead of touching him. That was his fault. The fact that he'd made her question herself around him, question what she meant to him—he was making everything clear today. As soon as they had some privacy. He still wanted to prove himself to her, but he couldn't go another second without letting her know what she was to him.

Taking the chance that she'd push him away, he wrapped his arm around her shoulders. He practically shuddered when she leaned into him, holding him tight. Her sweet scent teased him, drove his demon side crazy.

Ophelia looked between him and Rory as she pulled the door shut. The wolf shifter was almost two hundred years old—older even than her Alpha—but looked to be in her twenties. Petite and adorable with dark curly hair pulled up into a ponytail, her expression wasn't totally grim. He took that to be a good sign.

"She's been through a lot. She needs sleep and to feel safe. And she needs to start on a healthy diet. She's definitely malnourished. I'll come up with a good menu to start on immediately. For now, where is she going to stay?"

"Here, as long as she wants," Bo said.

"Good. She needs stability. These are some nice digs you've got." Her lips quirked up a fraction. "Never thought we'd find out where the mysterious Bo lived."

He just rolled his eyes. Until now no one except his sister and Nyx had known where his home was. He'd always liked it that way. After getting to know more of the Stavros pack though, he figured maybe having allies wasn't such a bad thing. Going through life looking at everyone like an enemy was exhausting.

"If you want to know anything else," she said, looking at Rory, clearly having picked up on the male's attachment to Liberty. "You need to ask her yourself. She doesn't want to talk about where she's from or who she is or how she got stuck in that realm. My advice, don't push her. Let her talk when she wants."

"I won't push," Rory rasped out, a sort of desperation in his gaze.

Yeah, Bo recognized that look. Shifters always got it when they were feeling overprotective of their mates. Bo could relate right about now because he was feeling obsessive and possessive where Nyx was concerned.

"Can I see her?" Rory continued.

Ophelia nodded. "Yeah. She was asking for you. I'm going to bring some food up in a bit for her. Make sure she eats a little bit of everything, but don't push her. She needs to have control."

"Okay." He was through the door before he'd finished speaking.

"Is he part of a pack?" Ophelia asked.

Bo shook his head. "No."

"Okay, well, I'll let Finn figure all that stuff out then, but I'm sure he won't mind your brothers in his territory. I'm gonna go whip something up in your kitchen. Nyx, you need a shower, food and sex. Doctor's orders." She winked before heading toward the stairs.

Bo wanted to kiss Ophelia. Figuratively.

When Nyx turned to look up at Bo her cheeks were flushed. "I don't know why she said that," she muttered.

"Because she's smart." Bo cupped Nyx's cheek, savored the feel of her soft skin.

Her pupils dilated as her breathing increased, but she kept her hands to herself. "I... don't know what you want from me, Bo." Confusion was etched on her expressive face.

"I know, and that's my fault." He stroked her cheek once. He just wasn't sure he should tell her that he wanted everything—that he wanted to completely possess her. Because he wasn't sure she'd want that, want him. Not completely anyway.

Her eyes went heavy-lidded for a moment but just as quickly she shook herself, took a small step back. "Then what happened before we ended up in that realm? I thought after you... went down on me..." She trailed off, her cheeks flushing again.

Just like that he got hard. It made him feel like a dick, but hearing those words from her and seeing the flush in her cheeks reminded him of how she'd looked when he'd made her come. "I behaved badly," he gritted out. He needed to just tell her, confess what an animal he was. She'd probably shove him away but she deserved to know the truth. "I was ready to take you right on the kitchen counter. Or the floor. You tasted fucking amazing and I just lost it. I would have been rough."

She stared at him, her breathing growing even more erratic. "Okay, so... you would have been rough. So what?"

"You're a virgin." He didn't even bother forming it as a question.

Nyx nodded. "Yes."

"I didn't care in that moment, I just wanted you and... you deserve better than a rough fucking on my kitchen counter, especially for your first time. You deserve... better than me." He rubbed the back of his neck. Even the thought of inadvertently being too rough, of hurting her, made him ache.

Her brow furrowed. "*That's* why you pushed me away? Because, what, you thought you might get too rough with me? I'm a freaking demigod, Bo. You won't break me."

"But—"

"*No.* I want you. A lot. I... kept coming up with reasons to push you away. *Valid* reasons, I might add, because my family is positively psychotic, but after being in that realm with you I've realized that we can both take care of ourselves. You're way more deadly that I realized. And, apparently so am I. So, I'm laying it out there. I'm open to more than friendship with you, but... make up your mind. Because if you start something then pull back again I might break your whole house." Her lips quirked up, her voice slightly teasing.

The tension inside him eased. She wasn't pushing him away. Not even close. "I want more than friendship with you too. Just *you.* I want to be exclusive." He'd never been in a long-term relationship, had never wanted to. Of course he wanted way more than a simple relationship with Nyx, but he figured he better start slow. He had a plan to seduce her, show her how good they were together, and make it so that she never wanted to leave him. He'd just get her addicted to him.

"Good. I won't share and... if you cheat on me there's no room for forgiveness." She looked nervous as she said it, wrapping her arms around her middle.

The fact that she felt the need to say that sliced at him. He knew what kind of reputation he had. One he'd earned and now hated. Not that he'd actually ever cheated on anyone. Impossible to do since he'd never been in a real relationship.

"You're mine, Nyx." He could feel his eyes lighting up, could see the glow illuminating her face ever so slightly. Damn it, he needed to play this smooth, but he couldn't hold back now. "Once we cross that line and commit, I'm not letting you go. So make sure this is what you want. That *I'm* what you want. I'm territorial and possessive and sometimes I'm going to act like a complete asshole where you're concerned. Not all the time, but... I'm going to get jealous and probably act stupid. And I'm a fucking half-demon, my bloodline isn't what you deserve. So make sure that's what you want. Because I won't let you go."

Wide-eyed, she nodded. "Okay." She looked as if she wanted to say more, but bit her bottom lip.

When it was clear she wasn't going to say anything else, he inwardly sighed. Yeah, maybe he'd come on too strong. Maybe she was hesitant now, needed time to think about it. Disappointment punched through him like a body blow but hell, he'd told her to think about it. He couldn't expect an answer right away.

He cleared his throat. "Listen, I've gotta go talk to Finn, see if he's really okay with more half-demons in his territory. And Cynara, Drake and Victoria are on their way over too. You want me to bring you some food up?"

Disappointment flickered over her face, but she shook her head. "I'm okay for now. I just want to grab a hot shower." Again, she looked as if she might say more, but didn't.

Damn it, he'd definitely come on too strong. "Okay." He didn't want to let her out of his sight even for a second, but knew that wasn't a viable option. He couldn't just drag her with him wherever he went. And his house was safe.

Didn't matter to his demon half. Right now he wanted to drag her into his arms, kiss her, but he headed for the stairs instead. If he got a taste of her now when he was all keyed up, they wouldn't be stopping. And that wasn't the way to win her over anyway. He needed to take things slow, not just jump her.

She needed to decide if he was the type of male she wanted. She'd seen his true form. Maybe once she thought about it she'd realize he wasn't the type of male for her.

Go take her now before she realizes what a monster you are, his demon half ordered.

Bo ignored the voice and went in search of Finn. It was the hardest thing he'd ever done. Especially when his demon side wanted to throw Nyx over his shoulder, take her to his room and forget the outside world existed for a few weeks.

* * *

Rory resisted the urge to pace and instead sat in the cushy armchair next to Liberty's bed. She was propped up against a bunch of pillows and wearing a long-sleeved pajama set. He wasn't sure if the clothes were

Nyx's or someone else's. Didn't matter, he'd be buying her anything she wanted. The realization that he wanted to take care of her, make her happy, was jarring when he knew nothing about her. Or very little.

It had been a long damn time since he'd been in the human realm. He normally wasn't here all that long either. He'd always thought humans were weak, pathetic.

Now that he was looking at one who'd survived unspeakable horrors, he knew he was an asshole for thinking that.

"Ophelia was nice?" he asked. His experience with other shifters hadn't been good. That being an understatement. But the healer had seemed as if she cared. And Bo seemed to trust Finn, the Stavros Alpha.

Liberty half-smiled, revealing a glimpse of just how stunning she was. "Yeah. She said I need food and sleep. I can deal with that." She cleared her throat, picked at the comforter. "Thank you for... doing what you did. For getting rid of those creatures." It was subtle, but a shudder wracked her slender frame.

He wanted to bring them back to life and kill them all over again for what they'd done to her. He could bathe in their blood, make them suffer for weeks. His canines pulsed against his gums, but he kept himself in check. For her. His wolf was feeling restless around her, wanting to comfort her. It was disturbing. He'd even bared his teeth at his brother earlier because he hadn't wanted Ian to carry her, something he'd never done. Not in true anger anyway. But he hadn't wanted anyone to touch her.

He just grunted a non-response to her thanks, not sure how to respond. He didn't want her gratitude.

"Is there someone you want to call?" Ophelia might have said not to push but he needed to make sure she didn't feel as if she was a prisoner here too.

"No. I just want to not think for a while. Does your brother really not mind if I stay here?" She pinned him with dark, haunted eyes. His wolf was going crazy with the need to erase the shadows there.

"He doesn't mind. And you're safe here." She'd always be safe as long as he was around. "If you want to go somewhere else just let me know. I'll make it happen." Right now he'd give everything to this female if it would help her heal. He was glad his new half-brother was letting them stay. His openness was surprising but Rory found he liked the guy.

She blinked in surprise. "Thank you. Can I ask you something?"

He nodded.

"How many different... uh, types of supernatural beings are there?"

He lifted a shoulder. "A lot. Shifters, vampires, half-demons, fae, and then there are mixes of every species, though that's a little rarer."

"Fae is like faeries, right?"

"Yeah."

"That's what Nyx is?"

He knew Liberty was asking because of Nyx's wings, which weren't visible in this realm. Not unless she wanted them to be. "Yeah." He also knew Nyx was more than a simple fae. She had some serious power she was keeping under wraps. And the whole transporting thing... he only knew of two beings who could do that. Gods and demigods. He was pretty sure she wasn't a goddess so that left one option. One of her parents must have mated with a fae.

"She's more though, isn't she?" Liberty whispered.

He nodded. "I think so."

"A few months ago I would have thought someone was crazy if they'd told me there were other realms and other beings besides humans in the world."

Rory filed that away. She couldn't have been in the Hell realm more than a few months if she said that. Of course that time frame would have felt like a lifetime, especially when held as a prisoner and abused in ways that made him want to rip something apart. "We've been around as long as humans."

She didn't respond, just picked at the comforter again. He couldn't tell if she was nervous or what. His experience with females was lacking. Hell, his experience with most species was lacking. After being basically rejected by his own pack, then other wolves, he'd had no problem retreating to an alternate realm.

Now guilt racked him that she'd been in his realm for who knew how long, suffering. And he'd done nothing. It didn't matter that he hadn't known. He and his brother had gotten complacent, just existing in their territory. They should have been out hunting predators, defending the weak. It was what their mothers had taught them. Instead they'd been selfish, only thinking of themselves.

"Do you want me to leave?" he asked quietly.

Liberty shook her head. "No. But I'm not really up for conversation. Ophelia gave me a couple pills, said they should help me sleep." Liberty nodded to a glass of water and two small pills on the nightstand. "But she said I should eat first."

He stood, glad to have a task. "I'll go check on the food then."

"You don't have to."

"I want to." Because the most primitive part of him needed to take care of her. He wasn't sure what to do with the odd feelings humming through him, but he would figure it out. For now he was going to go with his instinct.

And it was telling him to protect this female with his life.

CHAPTER FOURTEEN

Bo hurried up the stairs, probably too desperate to see Nyx. He didn't care. After talking to Finn about his brothers staying here, reassuring his sister that he wasn't going anywhere again and getting Ian settled in, he needed to see his... Nyx.

He didn't want to think of her as his mate. Not if she ended up rejecting him. Now that they were back in this realm and she had time to think about what a monster he was, he knew it was a possibility.

He knew he should hold off, but after he'd told her to make a decision, he wanted an answer. Too soon? Probably. *Yes.* But he apparently had no freaking control where she was concerned.

When he reached the door to her room, he stopped, took a deep breath. *Control.* He could show some. He just wanted to tell her goodnight. That was it.

He knocked softly once. Then again a little louder when she didn't answer. "Nyx?" Feeling a little like a stalker but not really caring he opened the door. Only because he was concerned. Something could have happened to her in the shower.

He snorted at himself. He couldn't even come up with believable lies to tell himself. Frowning, he looked around the empty room. Her bed hadn't been touched either and the light was off in the attached bathroom.

In full-on stalker mode, he headed to Ian's room. She wasn't there. Feeling a little guilty, but not enough to stop, he knocked on Liberty's door.

"Come in," a soft female voice called out.

He half-opened the door to find Liberty sitting up against a stack of pillow with one of his books opened against her lap and Rory at the foot of the bed in wolf form. The male lifted his head, made a snuffling sound before putting his massive head back on his paws. Damn, he'd never seen a wolf shifter so big.

Since Bo didn't want to come across as a stalker to them, he said, "Just checking on you, making sure you have everything you need."

"I'm great, thank you again. And listen, as soon as I can I'll pay you back for—"

"No. I don't want or need your money." He knew he sounded rude, but he needed to find Nyx.

She frowned at him, gave him a look that said this conversation wasn't over. It was for him but it was good to see a spark of determination in her gaze. "Well, thank you."

"You guys seen Nyx?" He tried to sound casual, but was pretty sure he failed.

When they both said no, he backed out and searched his entire fucking house. Nyx wasn't anywhere.

Full blown panic surged through him as he reached his bedroom door. Fuck this. He didn't care what he'd said about giving her time. He hadn't meant he wanted her to leave. His demon clawed at him, telling him to find her, bring her back where she belonged. What if her mother had grabbed her? It wasn't out of the realm of possibility that a goddess had gotten into his house undetected. That was pretty much the only type of being who could infiltrate his home without his permission.

He slung open his bedroom door, ready to grab his phone and start calling everyone who might know where Nyx was—and stopped dead in his tracks.

Nyx was on his bed with the covers pulled up to her chest. Her arms and what he could see of her chest were totally bare. One of the smaller lamps was on, the soft glow illuminating her perfectly.

She looked good in his bed. Perfect there. Just like that, he was hard.

Her midnight black hair was down, slightly damp as if she'd just taken a shower and her ocean blue eyes were as clear as he'd ever seen them. "I made my decision." Though her voice shook a fraction, he could see the truth in her gaze.

She wanted him and knew what it meant for him. This wasn't casual.

Without looking, he kicked the door shut behind him. If anyone tried to bother them, he'd probably destroy them. "Are you naked?" he rasped out.

Swallowing hard, she nodded.

"Drop the covers." He needed to see her more than he needed his next breath. His whole body practically vibrated with a desperate hunger.

Her fingers tightened on the cover once before she dropped it. He'd tasted her sweet pussy, had seen her mostly naked in the other realm but this was different. She was like an offering to him.

One he'd gladly take, devour, pleasure until she was sated and begging him to stop. "Lay back," he ordered, needing a semblance of control.

Nyx was completely naked, her pink nipples tight little buds and the sleek lines of her toned body absolute perfection. He'd never been more aroused. The urge to take her roughly was a primitive thing, but he shoved it back.

He needed her to come. More than once. It was her first time and even though he might not know anything about virgins, he knew that much. Which meant his clothes were staying on until that happened, because if he felt her bare breasts against his chest, or any other part of her against him, he'd lose it.

In the lagoon it had been hard enough to keep control when she'd been wrapped around him. Now there was nothing stopping them.

She stretched out on his bed, shoving at the covers with her feet so she was completely bared to him.

A low growl built in his throat. He stalked to the bed, climbed up it and covered her with his body. God, she felt good underneath him. Like the heaven he knew he'd never make it to. She was the only heaven he'd ever experience, and he had to savor it while he was still alive. What she'd said back in the Hell realm about him making her climax before they'd even kissed properly had bothered him. Yeah he'd kissed her before she'd gone into that camp but that was different. He'd been terrified he'd lose her.

Now he would take things slow, do this right. When she arched her back upward, wrapping her arms and legs around him, his control slipped faster than he'd expected.

He cradled her head in his palm before crushing his mouth to hers, taking everything she had to offer. She tasted sweet, perfect. Like *his*. Her tongue flicked against his and her fingers dug into his back with an urgency he felt all the way to his bones. He nipped at her bottom lip, tugged it between his teeth.

She moaned against him, the sound making his cock press insistently against his pants. Too fucking bad for him. This was all about her right now. She had to come before he got inside her.

He moved to her jaw, feathered kisses against the delicate line. "I'm gonna make you come against my mouth again." He nipped at her earlobe.

"I can live with that," she murmured, her voice breathy, teasing as her fingers trailed over his back.

Something inside him eased at her tone. This wasn't a race and she wasn't going anywhere, despite what the voice in his head said. His demon half wanted to lock her down, fuck for hours, completely claim her, but he could do this slow.

He smiled against the column of her neck, inhaled her sweet sunshine and roses scent.

Slow. Control.

He repeated the two words over in his head. He had this.

As he made his way down her tight body, he shuddered when he reached her breasts. Full, a little more than a handful, she had the most perfect pale pink nipples. He cupped them, staring down at her. None of his past experiences had had a sliver of the meaning this did.

"You're fucking mine," he growled before sucking one ripe bud into his mouth. He hoped she really understood that too. That she was his in every sense of the word. And vice versa. The female completely owned him. Until the day he died, he would be hers.

"Bo." She arched into him on a gasp, running her fingers through his short hair, digging into his scalp.

He savored the bite of pain, his dick pulsing even harder with the need to bury himself deep inside her. Nyx completely destroyed him. She made him want to be a better male, the type of male she'd be proud to call her own.

As he flicked his tongue over one of her tight buds, he memorized the way she reacted, the little sounds she made when he gently pressed his teeth against her nipple.

"That's good," she moaned, things around his room starting to rumble.

They were just getting started. He loved how reactive she was. He was vaguely aware of the sound of breaking glass, but ignored it. Until she stiffened under him. Hell no. "I don't care about it," he said against her skin, moving to her other breast. "Break the whole damn house."

God, he really did want to devour this female, lick and taste every sweet inch she had to offer.

The rumbling started again, making him smile against her other nipple. He needed her to let go, to trust him to take care of her. He pressed down with his teeth, tugged gently. She sucked in a breath and when he felt between her legs, barely stroked a finger through her folds, he shuddered.

She was soaked. And it was all for him. He slid a finger fully into her and she bucked against his hand. The female was so tight it shredded his control.

Almost.

Continuing a path of kisses down her stomach, he pulled his finger out, slid it in again.

"Bo." She moaned his name, rolling her hips in a way that made him want to throw his control out the window.

He moved lower, lower and sucked on her clit instead of teasing her. She jerked against him, her inner walls tightening around his finger. Oh, she liked that.

With his tongue he flicked and teased her sensitive bundle of nerves as he added another finger into her tight body.

Her fingers dug into his head again as she made the sweetest moaning sounds. She was already close, he could feel it with each stroke. And with each stroke he got even harder, something he hadn't thought possible. All he could imagine was her tight sheath wrapped around his cock instead and it was driving him to the brink of control.

"Oh..." She started rolling her hips faster so he increased the thrusting of his fingers and the pressure of his tongue.

Her inner walls contracted faster and faster until he felt the rush of her climax, her sweet release coating his fingers. He wasn't going to wait, guessed it would be better for her if he slid inside her while she was in the aftermath of her orgasm. And yeah, he needed to be inside her.

Moving faster than he'd even thought possible he stripped off his pants and T-shirt before he settled on top of her again.

Her eyes were heavy-lidded as she looked up at him. "That was amazing, but I want more." Her fingers trailed up his chest.

His cock lay heavy between them and even though he wanted nothing more than to push into her... "Do you need protection?" He realized he had no idea. Most supernatural beings didn't need to worry about condoms. They didn't have diseases and for shifters, at least females, they could only get pregnant a couple times a year. But Nyx was different.

The ghost of a smile teased her lips. "I'm good."

That was all he needed to know. Leaning down, he took her mouth again, this time softer, slower, with a marginal amount of control.

Surprising him, she reached between them, wrapped her fingers around his pulsing cock. Good, he wanted her to get used to the feel of him, know what to expect. As far as he was concerned, his cock was hers now.

He moaned into her mouth, slid his hand through the curtain of her hair, cupping the back of her head tight.

She lifted her hips and even though he didn't need the help, he let her guide him to her sweet, sweet entrance. When he pushed inside her he knew without a doubt that everything he'd experienced before paled in comparison to Nyx. Keeping his gaze pinned to hers, he went slowly, taking care with her until he was buried to the hilt. Not even his demon half was impatient now as he ordered him to do this right. Because fucking up with Nyx wasn't an option. Her inner walls were slick and oh-so-tight. He'd never felt anything more perfect.

Her eyes were wide, her pupils dilated and pure pleasure played across her face as she looked at him. In the past fucking had been just that. Now... watching her as he was completely buried inside her felt more intimate than anything he'd done.

"Move," she whispered. "I need more."

Propping up on his elbows, he pulled his hips back so that his cock barely breached her folds. No way could he pull out completely though. He simply wouldn't. Now that he'd had a taste, he didn't want to stop.

He pushed back in, growled when she arched into his thrust. The expression on her face was pure bliss. When he realized he wasn't remotely hurting her, he increased his pace, moving in and out of her with a near frenetic rhythm. His balls were pulled up tight, the need to come clawing at him.

When she buried her face against his neck, groaning as she came again, he finally let go. Her inner walls rippled around him as another climax overtook her. Aaaand, that was it. He wasn't holding back any longer. Not now. Joining her, he raked his teeth against her neck, teasing her soft, delicate skin. Just like shifters, his kind marked their mates.

But he held back. Barely.

He needed to ask first and not when he was buried balls deep inside her. Soon though, if she'd let him. He wanted to pierce her skin with his teeth, to let every supernatural being know she was taken. That she was his.

Groaning, he held her hips tight as he emptied himself inside her. He didn't think he'd ever come this hard. It had barely taken off the edge. The need for Nyx, for this female, was near obsession level. Or maybe he'd gone past that a month ago. Though he could go a few more rounds, he slowed and pulled back to look at her.

Smiling, she smoothed her fingers over his chest and watched him with bright, blue eyes.

"Did I hurt you?"

She snorted, the indelicate sound easing the tension in his chest. "Not possible. That was amazing. We should have been doing that a month ago."

Grinning, he skated his mouth over hers. "Then I guess we'll just have to make up for lost time," he murmured.

She nipped his bottom lip, her arms pulling him closer. "Definitely."

Even though every fiber of his being told him to stay inside her, to imprint himself on every part of her, he moved out of her and rolled to the side, pulling her tight against his chest.

Sighing, she wrapped her arms around him and nuzzled her face against his chest.

He gently stroked his fingers down her spine, surprised by how satisfied, how calm, he was just holding her, touching her. Yeah, he was completely gone for this female. If anyone tried to take her from him, he'd destroy them.

CHAPTER FIFTEEN

"It feels a little weird to be here," Nyx murmured as she and Bo arrived at his club. After a night—and morning and afternoon—of a lot of sex, he'd wanted to head here to see his employees and let everyone know he was okay. Cynara and Malloy had put in enough calls to pretty much everyone they knew that they were looking for knowledge of other realms in regards to Bo and her. Word had spread that something had happened to them. And Drake and Victoria had found a potential lead, but that was something he'd look into later. He needed to take care of his business first.

"We won't stay long," Bo said, giving her a look so heated she squirmed in her high heels. He'd changed his hair color tonight, something he hadn't done in a while. It was a wild blue and she loved it because it reminded her of what his skin looked like in demon form.

"I'm right next to you and I can scent the pheromones you're throwing off," Ian muttered as they reached the front door.

"I knew you were part shifter," Nyx murmured, nudging him with her elbow.

He pursed his lips. "And I know you're more than fae."

She just grinned. "It's true, I'm part fae, part awesome."

He blinked once, then laughed as Malloy yanked open the door. The huge ghoul ignored Nyx and Ian and pulled Bo into a giant hug.

Bo, clearly taken off guard, patted Malloy uncomfortably on the back and looked over at Nyx, his amber eyes pleading. As if she could help entangle him from the giant male.

"I'm glad you're back," Malloy said, stepping back, thumping him on the shoulder for good measure. He cleared his throat. "Cynara was worried about you."

Nyx covered a laugh. Right. Cynara.

"I missed you too. Malloy, this is Ian, my half-brother." He motioned to Ian as he grabbed Nyx's hand, pulled her close.

She loved that he wasn't letting her out of his sight and had to be touching her at all times. Because she felt exactly the same way. She was all in with him. Bo was hers and she wanted the whole world to know.

Malloy shook hands with Ian, nodding politely, but his eyes widened when he saw Bo and Nyx's linked hands. Then his grin expanded to ridiculous proportions. "'Bout fucking time." His grin faded as he tapped his ear piece. "All right, let me know if you need backup…"

Bo just nodded at him, letting him get back to work, and ushered her and Ian into the very full club.

"Nice place, brother." Ian glanced around taking in the various bars, the scantily-clad wait staff, the various supernatural beings who were either on the dance floor, at one of the bars or in any number of the seating areas.

Nyx grinned when she saw Cynara slide off the seat by a high-top table, champagne *bottle* in hand. She ran at them, arms open wide, and practically tackled the three of them in a giant all-encompassing hug, ending with a smacking kiss on Nyx's cheek.

"I can't believe I have two more brothers!" At that she chugged straight from the expensive bottle before showing off her fangs in a big smile.

Nyx blinked. "Are you drunk?" She'd never seen Cynara even tipsy.

"You better believe it! Hey, where's my other brother?" she demanded, looking between the three of them, her purple eyes flaring brighter.

"Ah, he won't leave the human female," Ian said. Again with that note of concern for Rory. Nyx had noticed it in the cave but wasn't sure what it was about.

"I'll stop by and see them both later then. Oh." She whirled to Bo, a flurry of activity in her inebriated state. "Some skanks are here asking for you, wanted to know if you'd join them for some drinks. I told them to suck a bag of dicks."

"She is who you learned that expression from?" Ian's eyebrows rose as he looked at Nyx.

She just lifted a shoulder, trying to ignore that some females had been asking for Bo. Of course they were. He was an attractive male and he'd had an active sex life before her. Very active, apparently. It shouldn't bother her, but it did. Not that she judged him, she just hated the thought of anyone but her touching him. Especially when her experience was so lacking. He didn't seem to have any complaints though if his ridiculous stamina was any indication. Still... she worried he'd get bored with her. And what if he had feelings for one of those females?

"Spread the word that I'm taken." There was a bite to Bo's words as he wrapped a possessive arm around Nyx's shoulders.

Cynara's eyes widened as she looked at the two of them. "'Bout fucking time," she said, mirroring Malloy.

"I agree." Bo kissed the top of Nyx's head, the simple action heating her up from the inside out and dispelling her worry. "Is there anything I need to be aware of tonight or can we grab a table?" he asked his sister.

"As far as I know, we're all good. Now let's get some more drinks and hit the dance floor." She hooked her arm through Ian's. "I can find you some nice females," she said, her voice trailing off as she dragged him with her.

"She's hilarious," Nyx murmured, leaning into Bo's hold as they followed after them through the throng of people. The music was thumping and the scent of sex, alcohol and perfumes filled the air. She turned her face into Bo's chest, inhaling the unique scent that was all him, the masculine notes to it eclipsing everything else.

"Yes, but... Cynara drinks maybe once or twice a year. This might not be good."

"Should we do... anything?" Cynara was a grown woman—an eighty-two year old half-vamp, half-demon—who could take care of herself, but still, if Bo was worried Nyx wondered if she should be too.

"No, she's... fine." But he didn't sound sure.

Bo was never unsure about anything. "She's probably just excited to have new brothers."

"Maybe. The last time she got drunk it was because her asshole ex showed up here." He shook his head, as if clearing cobwebs and placed another kiss on her forehead as they reached the high-top table where Ian and Cynara were sitting.

Nyx hadn't realized Cynara had an ex. At least not one worth getting drunk over. She seemed immune to the opposite sex. Before they'd even sat, one of Bo's vampire security appeared as if out of nowhere. He leaned down to Bo's ear, murmuring too low for Nyx to hear but she could tell by Bo's annoyed expression that he was going to have to deal with work stuff.

Sliding onto one of the chairs, she squeezed his hand when he gave her an apologetic look. "Go, do your thing. This place would fall apart without you."

He leaned close, nipped her bottom lip. "Be good without me."

"No promises," she murmured teasingly.

His eyes went supernova. "No dancing without me then."

She wouldn't dance with another male anyway. She didn't want anyone but Bo, but knowing how territorial he was, she definitely wouldn't. "As long as you don't without me."

"Deal. I'll only be five minutes, max." Bo looked at Ian, gave him a hard look that wasn't difficult to decipher. But she thought he was silently telling Ian to look out for her.

She decided not to remind either of them that she was a freaking demigod and had literally made a guy explode just yesterday.

Feeling a little bit like a lovesick maniac, she watched as Bo disappeared into the crowd before turning back to the others. To her surprise there was already a new bottle and thankfully glasses at the table.

"So, you and Bo are finally together," Cynara practically squealed. Definitely out of character for the female. Her purple hair was in a complicated twist at the back of her neck tonight, showing off her sharp cheekbones.

Nyx felt her cheeks warm up as she grinned. "Yep." They were definitely together.

Cynara shook her head. "I thought he'd never work up the courage to make a move."

Nyx cleared her throat, unsure what to say. She adored Cynara but didn't really want to talk about her and Bo, especially not in front of his siblings. Her friend Keelin had once told Nyx that there was no such thing as TMI when it came to shifters, but she somehow doubted Cynara or Ian wanted to hear her gush about things between them. "Well, he did and I'm going to have some of that champagne." She picked up the new bottle and started pouring a glass for Ian and herself since Cynara was still apparently drinking out of her own bottle. "So what did we miss in the past couple days?"

"No way! I want to hear about you and Bo."

"Well I do *not*," Ian said in his slightly raspy Irish accent. "I heard them enough last night."

Nyx's eyes widened, her cheeks burning. "You didn't?"

He just snorted and chugged his drink in one gulp.

She covered her face with her hands while Cynara giggled uncontrollably.

"Okay, fine, no details," Cynara finally said. "I don't need to hear about that anyway. But what happened to like, make you guys get sucked into another realm? Bo was pretty vague on the specifics. I know that Victoria and Drake might have found a lead on a..." She glanced around then leaned forward, "stolen wormhole package," she whispered.

Nyx didn't know more than that. The only thing she was certain of was that she'd delivered her mother's package and she'd covered her end of their stupid bargain. As far as she was concerned, she was completely done with her mother—and her entire family. And she'd never be going back to that cemetery again. "Ah, we're not really sure. It was like something triggered it."

"It's crazy that you ended up in a realm with Ian and Rory." She patted Ian's cheek adoringly, the almost motherly action so at odds with the female Nyx had gotten to know. "Still can't believe I have new brothers."

Ian actually blushed. "You're gonna kill my game here tonight," he muttered.

But Nyx could tell he wasn't serious. He hadn't even looked at any females since he'd come in here.

"Good. I was just kidding earlier anyway. There aren't any nice girls here. Besides Nyx of course."

Ian just grinned, starting to respond when a loud commotion made Nyx turn to look over her shoulder. Two of the high tabletops were upended and a group of four males were shoving at each other. Typical Friday night.

The crowd around them parted, giving Nyx a perfect view of Bo.

And the blonde female draped over him as if she owned him. Her arm was around his shoulders, her breasts pressed up against him as she leaned up to talk in his ear. Bo's jaw was clenched tight, and it was clear he was annoyed. She knew he wouldn't cheat on her, but... Nyx's champagne glass shattered in her hand, even as she tried to tell herself to get it together, to keep herself under control. Turning away from the sight, she found Cynara looking pissed as she saw what Nyx had just seen.

Nyx knew she should march up to the blonde female, say something, but if she did, she was likely to bring this whole club down on everyone's heads if she couldn't keep her emotions under control. Hurting a bunch of innocent people wasn't something she ever wanted to do. She knew Bo wasn't cheating, that he was just dealing with some female. That much was clear by his body language. Didn't mean she had to sit here and watch.

She placed the broken stem on the table and slid off her seat. Ian started to follow her, but she shoved him back with her powers, surprising even herself with the action. The last thing she saw before she disappeared into the crowd was his stunned expression.

Nyx pushed back the thread of guilt worming its way through her, but she just needed some space outside for a few minutes. And she didn't want a babysitter. Without getting a few breaths of air, she was likely to hurt a ton of people. After she got herself under control, she'd talk to Bo.

* * *

"Damn it," Bo muttered, shoving the female away from him as Nyx disappeared into the crowd. He'd tried to be polite, not wanting to hurt her ego in front of her pridemates, but the feline shifter wasn't listening. No one touched him against his will.

And no one hurt Nyx. Which he was afraid *he'd* just done.

"Hey! What the fu—"

He felt his eyes brighten as he faced the blonde, could feel his beast clawing at him, telling him to chase after Nyx right the fuck now. "I told you I was taken. Twice. I told you not to touch me. Get out of my club. You're banned." Ignoring her cries of indignation, he motioned to Malloy, who was hurrying his way. "Get rid of them. Now. Use a side exit."

Not bothering to be polite, he shoved his way through the crowd until people just parted the way for him. He was seriously close to letting go and shifting to his demon form in the human realm. Something he'd never done in public. Right now he didn't care.

He yanked the front door open, letting it fall behind him with a thud. It was immediately quieter, all the sounds from inside dimming but he couldn't see or hear Nyx... "Nyx!"

"I'm right here," she muttered.

He swiveled to see her leaning against the outer wall, arms crossed over her chest, looking frustrated. She'd worn high heels, tight jeans and a filmy, feminine top that showed off all her delectable cleavage. "I wasn't—"

"I know." Her jaw was tight, her expression annoyed as she looked at him.

He wanted to take her into his arms, but held off, standing in front of her instead. Her sweet scent was making him crazy. "I told that female I was taken but she didn't listen." Something he'd never had a problem with before. Not in his own club. Of course, before Nyx, he'd never really said no to anyone.

"She's one of your former... lovers?" Damn it, was that hurt in her voice?

"I... we had sex once. Over a year ago. Maybe longer. It meant nothing and I barely remember her." He barely remembered anyone before Nyx. "You're mine, Nyx. I don't want anyone else." God, he wanted to hold her, but her arms were still crossed over her chest.

"I know. I just got angry and didn't want to destroy your club because I couldn't handle my emotions. I understand you've had former relationships. I just didn't like seeing someone touching what was mine."

Which was insanely hot, even if he knew now wasn't the appropriate time to tell her that. He liked that she was territorial because he sure as hell was. He should let it go because he didn't want to talk about his past, but he knew they needed to get this out in the open now. Get it over with. "First, I've never had an actual relationship. I've only fucked people."

When she winced he wanted to kick his own ass, but continued. "If I could go back and change how I was before I met you, I would. But I can't. Sex and fighting are the only things that keep my demon at bay in this realm. Until you."

Her arms loosened a fraction. "What do you mean?"

He stepped a little closer, placing his hands on either side of her head against the building. "As soon as I met you, I felt different. I don't know what it is and I don't really need to question it. All I know is, you're mine. And I'm yours. I'm sorry you had to see someone touching me like that." She'd seen a partial video of him kissing someone last month during an investigation and he'd never forget the hurt on her face then. The truth was, if he saw her kissing someone, touching someone, he'd lose his shit. She showed more restraint than he ever could.

She gently placed her hands on his chest. "I feel like I have no right to get jealous. Not really. But it sucks knowing you have so much experience." Her expression was so raw, vulnerable, it sliced him up. "I worry maybe... I won't be enough."

Fuck it, he gathered her into his arms. The desperate need to hold her, comfort her, outweighed giving her any space. "I never imagined someone like you existed, Nyx. And definitely not for me. I feel like I've been living in a haze until I met you." He wondered if he sounded as dumb as he felt admitting all this. "I know I'm not good enough for you so I get your fears because I have them too. I'm terrified you'll wake up one day and realize you can do so much better than me." Admitting that out loud took way more courage than he'd imagined. He didn't want her to know these things.

"Oh, Bo..." Shaking her head, she cupped his cheek, her hand soft. He leaned into it, savoring the feel of her touching him. "That's never going to happen. I think we both just have to get used to being in a relationship and everything that comes with it."

He nodded, his grip on her tightening. He started to respond when the door flung open and Cynara walked out, her eyes wide.

Bo froze when a tall, dark-haired familiar looking man stepped out with her, a knife at her back, right where her heart was. It had to be a silver dagger. For a moment, his heart stopped.

The male had been in Bo's club before, had threatened Nyx. His ears were just slightly pointed, giving away his heritage.

"What the hell are you doing, Kato?" Nyx stepped forward, but Bo snagged an arm around her waist, held her close.

He filed the name Kato away because this male was going to die one way or another.

"You refuse to listen to your father's summons, so I've been sent to fetch you." He said it so offhandedly, his tone dripping with derision.

"You think threatening my friend is going to make that happen?" She didn't try to step forward again, but she nudged Bo with her elbow.

The male smiled evilly, dug the blade into Cynara's back a fraction. His sister gritted her teeth and he knew she was refusing to make a sound. But he could tell she was in pain. "This is just a bonus. Come with me and no one gets hurt."

"Fine."

"Nyx—"

"I'm going." Her gaze snapped to Bo's, fire and anger burning there. "Just trust me," she murmured. His grip on her tightened as she turned back to the male who was a walking dead man. "I'll go if you agree not to hurt or target Bo or any of his siblings. Ever."

The male's eyes narrowed a fraction. "As long as they don't attack me, I agree."

"Swear it."

"I swear."

Bo wasn't worried about some pussy fae coming after him and he wasn't letting Nyx go without him. "I'm going with you."

"No." Nyx tried to step away from him, but he held her tight to him. "Don't do this," she growled.

"We're a package deal."

She let out a growl of frustration, then to his surprise flung him away without touching him. But he felt the force of her power as he flew through the air, slamming against the side of the building. He barely felt the impact, was just pissed she was leaving without him. Damn, stubborn female.

The fae male immediately shoved Cynara away.

"Nyx, don't go with him!" Cynara shouted.

"Can you guys just trust me?" Nyx demanded, grabbing the fae male by the forearm.

Bo jumped up, raced at them but they disappeared in a whirlwind of noise that died almost immediately. He roared, his beast about to break free when Ian stormed out with three males. All fae, given the slight point to their ears.

"Found this garbage sneaking around your place." He pointed a sword at them. "Get the hell out of here."

One of the males stepped forward. "My sword—"

"Is now my property. Get. Out. Of. Here."

"Now," Bo added, growling deep in his throat. "Your friend got what he came for." And would die very soon because of it. Bo wasn't actually sure these fae were with the male who'd come for Nyx but it couldn't be a coincidence that they were here tonight. Because fae didn't frequent his place, much less four of them in one night.

The males turned and practically ran across the parking lot. Bo wanted to chase after them, destroy them, but he had more important stuff to take care of. Like finding Nyx.

"Bo," Cynara started, but he held up his hand and pulled his cell phone out. He quickly dialed a familiar number.

"Hey," Finn answered on the first ring. "I'm headed to your place now."

"Three fae males just left my place. I'm guessing they don't have permission to be in your territory. I'm not sure where they're headed."

Finn growled, low and deadly. "I'll find them." He ended the call before Bo could respond.

Not that he needed to anyway. That was one problem solved. Now he needed to take care of another.

"What are you planning?" Cynara demanded, standing in front of him with her hands on her hips. Gone was his tipsy sister. Her eyes were clear and worried. "I don't like that look."

"I'm going after Nyx." He just had to find out where the hell she'd gone.

"She said to trust her. Her father won't hurt her, you know that."

"No, he just wants to marry her off." And the fae prince was coming between Bo and his mate. That was the only thing his demon half registered. Wherever Nyx had gone, he was going too. He just had to figure out how to get there.

Then he was bringing her home where she belonged—and mating with her. He wasn't waiting any longer to make things official. If she'd be his mate, he was claiming her. Every supernatural being would know she was taken.

* * *

Victoria waited impatiently as her phone rang. "Pick up, pick up," she muttered.

"Victoria?" Arya's supermodel face came on the screen, frowning. Probably because the ancient dragon shifter didn't trust the cell phone—or any technology. She said it was unnatural. "Can you see me?"

"Yes. Listen, I know you've been trying to reach out to Nyx's father to…" She cleared her throat, unsure how to phrase it. Arya wanted to make it clear to Nyx's prince father that if he tried to force Nyx into anything, he'd go to war with the Petronilla dragon clan. Because apparently thousands of years in Protective Hibernation hadn't dulled Arya's bloodthirst. At least according to Keelin, who wanted to take a more diplomatic approach. "So have you reached him?"

She sniffed haughtily. "That child has been ignoring my requests for a meeting. I'm at the end of my patience."

Only she would consider a two hundred-plus-year-old prince a child. Victoria shook her head. "Well we need to do something. Bo just called in a frenzy because Nyx was taken—sort of, she did transport herself willingly—to see her father. He's ready to go to war with the fae but he's not sure how to get to her father's realm. I don't think it's such a good idea for him to go after her anyway, but I thought if you could find where she was, maybe... we could do something that wouldn't involve violence and bloodshed."

Arya's eyes went pure predator and Victoria wasn't ashamed to admit the female terrified her in that moment. "I will get back to you, but... her father isn't in the fae realm. He's in London." She set the phone down but must have forgotten to hang up because Victoria heard her shout, "Dragos, we might get our fae war after all." Her tone was gleeful.

Victoria pressed the end call button because she definitely didn't need to hear anymore. "Your mother is terrifying," she muttered, glancing over at Drake who'd stayed out of sight during the call. If he hadn't, Arya would have insisted on having a twenty minute conversation with him and right now they didn't have that kind of time.

He slid down the couch and pulled her into his lap. "I know."

226 | KATIE REUS

"I know you heard what she said. We need to call Bo."

Drake's smile dimmed. "He's going to want to go to London immediately."

"I'll ask Finn if Bo can use his plane."

"I could just fly him."

Victoria's eyebrows rose. "You would to that?"

He lifted a shoulder. "I like the half-demon. And it's for Nyx. I'm not sure if it's wise though. We still don't know who stole the wormhole package."

Victoria frowned. "I think we have a pretty good idea." Even if she couldn't prove it. Nyx's mother was the one who'd given Nyx that package to deliver, and since Chaos was a goddess, she had the ability to erase memories. Victoria was only surprised she'd let Thurman and the vampire live.

"Yeah," Drake murmured. "Let's call Bo then."

Whatever they decided to do, she voted for the private plane. Riding her dragon mate all the way to London did not sound like fun, even if he was always careful.

CHAPTER SIXTEEN

Nyx was barely containing her rage, but she managed to keep her expression neutral as she followed Kato down the long, polished marble tile hallway of her father's mansion. She'd originally taken them to the fae realm but apparently her father was currently in his London home. So they'd come here and she was at the end of her rope.

She was going to hash things out with her father, then return to Bo. He'd definitely be pissed that she'd just left like that, but she didn't need anyone to fight her battles. Definitely not this one. And his presence would have just made things worse. She planned to be diplomatic and end things now. It was time her father knew he had no control over her and never would.

"It will just be a few minutes," Kato said as they reached a sitting room. Her father's office was behind two eight foot high intricately carved wood doors.

"It will be now or I leave." Okay, so much for being diplomatic.

Before Kato could respond, one of the doors opened and her father stepped out. He nodded at her once. "Nyx."

"Linos." Because no way on this realm or any other was she calling him dad, daddy, father or any freaking other parental title. He was lucky she called him by his name and not what she thought of him. But… diplomacy. She could show it.

She wanted to end things here so that he retained some of his pride. Because she knew that if she damaged his fragile ego it could come back to hurt others in her life later.

His lips pulled into a thin line as he stepped back. "So nice of you to finally arrive."

She didn't give Kato another look as she strode past her father and into his expansive office. She knew he did a lot of business in the human realm, but wasn't sure exactly what it was. She just knew he was filthy rich in this realm and his own.

"Your mate-to-be has picked a venue for your wedding. He prefers it to be in our realm. But if you would like to have your dress made in the human realm that is acceptable. The menu choices have already been made…" He continued droning on, not bothering to greet her in any real way, not that she'd expected it, but it still pissed her off. And he just started telling her what she was going to do, as if he truly thought she was going to go through with his insane arranged marriage.

Ignoring him as he talked, she strode over to his minibar and eyed the bottles. Knowing it would annoy him more than anything, she made a drink for herself. Vodka on the rocks with a slice of fresh lime.

Tumbler in hand she sat in one of his uncomfortable chairs and crossed her legs. "Are you quite done?" she asked, cutting him off midsentence.

He just stared at her, wide-eyed, his blue eyes so much like her own, it annoyed her. She hated that she'd gotten most of her looks from him. Not his height though, because the male was truly tall in the way the fae were. All elegant and willowy.

"I'm most certainly not done," he snapped. Before he could continue, the door opened and Kato strode in, his expression grim.

"Apologies, sire. Three of your males have been... killed. The Stavros Alpha cut off all their heads."

Nyx snorted, earning a glare from both of them. "You should have asked for permission to enter his territory. You broke the common rule of pretty much all supernatural beings. If you attempt to retaliate you will go to war with not only his pack but the Marius vampire coven."

Because Finn had mated a powerful bloodborn. It didn't matter that Lyra wasn't part of her coven anymore, the vamps who now ran it would do anything she asked. And if she requested they go to war with some fae. They'd do it. Gleefully. Because fae tended to be snobbish assholes. It was no wonder her mother had mated with a fae prince. They really were cut from the same cloth.

"You need to speak to the prince with more respect," Kato snapped, straightening to his full six foot three height.

"Oh, get off your high horse," she snapped, letting the leash of her control go. Using her growing gift, she flung him back against a case of built-in wood bookshelves. They cracked under the impact.

The only thing she felt remotely bad about was that she might have damaged a couple books.

Kato snarled. "You stupid—"

"Enough!" Linos pointed at the door. "Get out. Nyx is royalty and no matter your feelings, you will speak to her with respect."

Nyx wasn't exactly surprised. Her father was all about the class system. He wasn't ordering Kato out because of a sense of any type of loyalty to her specifically.

Kato shot her a dark glare and shut the door behind him. Nyx stood, downing her drink in a gulp because she knew it would offend her father. She slammed the glass onto his desk with a rude flourish. Apparently she simply didn't have the capacity to be diplomatic today.

"I'm going to leave and neither you nor anyone under your purview will come after me ever again. I'm cutting our ties completely today. I will not be marrying anyone you choose, or living in the fae realm, or anywhere you think I should."

When he flew to his feet, his face mottled with rage, she placed her hands on his desk, leaned forward. "I've put up with your tiresome demands because I couldn't be bothered by you." Not exactly true, she'd been worried he would come after Bo or others she cared for.

Now that she'd started to come to terms with what she could do, no one was going to hurt the people in her life. Not while she still had breath in her lungs. All around the office priceless vases and other glass pieces started shattering as she stared at him. "You've never treated me like a daughter. You've never treated me like anything that matters."

"Your mother and I had a deal!"

"You didn't have one with me. If you bother me again I will raze this house to the ground. Then I will destroy the rest of your properties, in *every* realm. After that, I'll start getting creative." She mentally ripped one of the bookshelves from the wall, inwardly smiling when he jumped back, flinching from the destruction.

"Are we clear?"

He didn't respond, just stared at her with a new kind of horror.

The sight of it made her way happier than it should have. "Answer me."

"You are just like your mother," he spat.

Nyx narrowed her eyes. "I'm nothing like *either* of you."

He drew a deep breath, straightened. "I will not bother you again." He was going for neutral, but she heard the rage underlying his words.

"Swear it." Because the fae were big on promises. If he gave his word and then broke it she'd be within all her legal rights to pretty much destroy him and everything he owned.

"I swear. You're a fool for throwing away such a prized marriage. Don't think I don't know it's for that half-demon. He'll use you and discard you in less than a month. Demons are not capable of being faithful," he spat. "Now get out of my sight."

Feeling an immense sense of relief, she didn't respond, just transported back to the parking lot of Bo's club. She'd only been gone for about an hour.

Even though she knew he'd be mad she was so glad she'd finally taken care of her father. He might try to get back at her later, but she'd be ready for him. She wasn't going to live her life in fear.

Malloy opened the front door, smiling when he saw her. "Bo's gonna be so glad to see you. You okay?" He ran a quick gaze over her.

"I'm good. Where is he?"

"Behind the red door. In room five." He tapped his ear. "I'd tell him you're here but he doesn't have his earpiece in."

After murmuring "thanks" she made her way around the crowd so she wouldn't have to fight her way through everyone. She would not jump to any conclusions about him being behind the red door. He owned the place, of course he'd have to take care of work-related issues. Still, that insecure little voice in the back of her head told her she'd never be good enough. Her father's words rang in her head, but he was wrong. Bo would be faithful.

* * *

Ten minutes earlier

"What?" Bo demanded as Cal, one of his vampire employees, stuck his head in the doorway of Bo's office.

"There's been an incident in one of the private rooms."

"Take care of it," he snarled, his cell phone up to his ear. He'd called in too many favors to count in the last hour trying to get a bead on Nyx's family. Turned out her father owned property all over the world and was, according to Drake's mother, in the human realm right now. Bo was going to catch a flight out as soon as he could make it. Victoria said they could use her pack's private jet, but he was going to see if he could get out of here faster.

"It's Janae and Myla. Some asshole cut up Myla pretty bad. Janae's a wreck and—"

Ah, hell. "I'm coming," he said as Victoria said, "Hey... what?" on the other end of the line.

Bo nodded at Cal as he rounded the desk, but continued talking to Victoria. "I wasn't talking to you. How long will it take to get your pack's pilot ready to go?"

"Already done. Finn said he's on the way to the airport now. Want us to pick you up? It's on the way."

"Yeah, thanks. Meet you outside in ten." He disconnected as he exited into the club from his private hallway of offices and storage rooms. "What happened?" he demanded.

"They brought in a new partner tonight, never been to the club before. But he knew the rules. Guess he thought he could get rough with the girls and we wouldn't do anything. Myla's healing fine, but they're both upset."

"Where's the asshole?" Bo glanced out at the club, scanned it for any trouble as they headed to the red door.

"Cynara's got him in holding," Cal said, his voice grim.

Good. "Species?"

"Vampire."

"He knew the rules for certain?"

"Yep. Malloy went over everything with him since he was a newcomer. Had him sign a disclaimer, we ran his full background. He agreed to everything on video and signed in blood. Knew the room would be monitored since he was new."

So the dumbass thought he could hurt someone on Bo's property? Rage surged through him. "Coven?" he asked, yanking open the private, red door.

He didn't have time to deal with this shit, but Myla and Janae were two avian shifters and regulars. He wasn't certain of their exact species but they weren't as strong as most shifters and they were sweet. Though they were mates, they liked to come to his club and pick up a third member to join them. They only used his place because they felt safe here. Everyone knew his reputation, knew what would happen if they broke the rules. It was why he had people sign in blood.

"None."

"Have Cynara dispatch him. Or you can do it." He didn't care who killed the male. Normally he'd take care of it himself, but there wasn't time tonight. Considering the mood Cynara seemed to be in tonight maybe it'd make her feel better to kill some bastard.

When they reached room number five, Bo didn't have to open the door since it was already half-open.

Cal stood back and tilted his head back to the way they'd come. "I'm gonna help Cyn take care of this guy. We'll make an example out of him." His expression was dark, unforgiving.

Bo didn't blame him. Myla and Janae were adorable shifters who never caused any trouble. Hurting one of them was the equivalent of hurting a freaking puppy. When he stepped inside, one of his security guys was standing near the bed, murder in his gaze.

He stepped forward. "Boss—"

"It's being taken care of," he murmured as he crouched down in front of the females who were half-naked, crying and holding on to each other on the edge of the bed. They didn't need to hear one of his employees going on a rage-fueled rant. Even if Bo could totally relate.

When Myla looked up at him, he had to forcibly push his own anger back when he saw the claw marks across the left side of her face. "I'm so sorry, Myla." He lifted a hand to his security guy, but didn't take his gaze off the females. "Get a first aid kit. Now." They'd be healed within the next hour or two but he still wanted to take care of this as much as he could.

"He seemed like such a nice guy." Janae wiped at wet cheeks with her free hand, keeping her other arm around Myla's shoulders.

Myla sniffled and swiped at her own tears. "Until I told him that we wouldn't be tied up. We didn't know that freak well enough..." More tears spilled down her cheeks and she turned into Janae's embrace.

Ah, hell. "I'm so sorry, guys. That fucker is being taken care of as we speak. He won't hurt anyone again." Bo reached out, pulled them both close into an embrace. His demon half didn't particularly like touching another female, but he needed to comfort them both right now. They needed to know they were safe, okay.

His hug seemed to calm them down. He kissed the top of Myla's head, then Janae's—and turned at a shuffling sound.

Nyx stood there, her eyes wide with hurt and full-on anger like he'd never seen. Her normally ocean blue eyes were storm clouds.

"Nyx—"

"Fuck you!" She transported faster than he'd ever seen, leaving a wake of destruction in her path. The ceiling and door splintered, plaster and wood raining down on them until he stopped everything midair, moved the pieces back into place on autopilot.

Fuck, fuck, fuck. He had to get out of here. Find Nyx. Now.

"Oh, Bo..."

He turned to see Myla and Janae looking at him with horrified, sympathetic expressions. "Everything's okay," he said as Dmitry returned, first aid kit in hand.

"Oh God, please don't let Nyx think..."

He shook his head, standing. "Don't worry about anything else except yourselves right now. I've gotta go but I'll see you guys soon. I'll make up for what happened to you here, I promise." It didn't matter that everyone signed an agreement, that they understood the risks of using his rooms, he still looked out for his people.

The hurt he'd seen in Nyx's eyes was worse than the anger. It sliced at his insides deeper than anything he'd ever experienced. Worse than the pain he'd felt the first time he'd met his father and realized what a monster the male truly was, worse than getting the shit beat out of him by the bastard. Instead of going through the club, he used one of the back exits. He'd just pulled the door open when his phone buzzed in his pocket. Cool, spring air rushed over him as he stepped outside.

He didn't want to talk to anyone right now but when he saw the number of one of his burner phones on the caller ID, he answered. It had to be one of his brothers. "Yeah?"

"Hey," Rory murmured. "Your girl is here and she's upset. Damn near destroyed your kitchen in her transport. Won't say what's wrong but she headed up-stairs. Is everything okay?"

"Don't let her leave. No matter what. If you have to, hold on to her. You and Ian both." Ian had headed back to Bo's place not long after Nyx had left an hour ago. "She can't transport without taking you." He hung up, not bothering to tell his brother anything else. Mainly because he was barely hanging on to his control right now, was barely hanging on to his human form.

Nyx could literally go anywhere she wanted in the blink of an eye. She could leave him. Forever. Panic pulsed through him with every breath he dragged in, with every step he took.

He'd get to her before she left. He had to.

CHAPTER SEVENTEEN

"Rough transport?" Ian's raspy voice made Nyx look up from her open suitcase.

Normally she was a freak about keeping things organized but she was just tossing things in, barely keeping her chaos in check. For a moment she thought the room was trembling, that she'd completely lost it and Bo's house would soon crumble around her—but it was just her hands shaking.

Screw it, if she left something behind she'd just replace it. She didn't want to stay here a second longer than necessary. "Yeah, sorry, didn't mean to scare you guys," she muttered, turning away from the bed and heading into the bathroom. Ugh, why was he here talking to her? Couldn't he see that she wanted to be left alone?

"Where'd you go earlier? How'd things go with your father? Bo said the guy demanded to see you or something?" he asked from the doorway.

She was surprised Ian was being all chatty. Without looking at him, she started tossing all her makeup and other stuff into her pink and black toiletry bag. "Things went fine," she snapped, then winced. "Ah, sorry. Listen, Ian, I don't feel like talking right now."

"Yeah, I can see that." Arms crossed over his massive chest, he watched her curiously. "What's going on, because last I heard you and Bo were an item? Now you're leaving and you look as if you want to murder someone."

Well she certainly wasn't going to tell Ian that she caught his brother with not one, but two females. Her heart actually ached as the scene played in her mind. She'd been gone for an hour. One, single hour.

And when she came back from her father's, Bo wasn't worried about her, wasn't out trying to find her. It didn't matter that she'd told him to trust her, that she would take care of things, she'd still expected him to be worried or mad at her. Or... something.

Instead he'd had his arms wrapped around two naked females—in one of his private rooms. She'd heard him murmuring to them, all soft. A burst of rage and jealousy slid through her, sharp and spiky. What if she'd known the females? His body had been blocking them so she hadn't gotten a good look at their faces, but if it was someone she was friendly with... ugh.

Crack.

The bathroom mirror cracked right in the middle, the breaks spidering out in all directions, as if she'd slammed her fist into it. She wished she had. Scratch that, she wished she'd slammed her fist right into Bo's handsome face.

"I don't live here. Never did," she finally muttered, zipping up her bag. When she went to move past Ian, he just stood there, his eyebrows raised.

"Move."

Lips pursed, he stepped aside. "Come on, Nyx, talk to me. Whatever happened between you guys, it can't be that bad."

She was pretty much at her capacity for niceness. She just wanted to be alone to mourn what a jackass Bo was and what a fool she'd been. She couldn't believe him. Gah, she couldn't believe she'd fallen for his lies. As his words from just an hour ago replayed in her mind she felt her rage building again.

With shaking hands, she slammed her suitcase shut. When she tried the zipper she couldn't get it to zip. Only when Ian covered her hands did she stop.

"I'll get it," he said quietly, zipping it up. "I'll carry it downstairs for you too. You need to talk to Liberty before you leave."

Dang it, he was right. Nyx hadn't been thinking about anyone else but herself. She couldn't leave without giving Liberty a way to contact her or saying goodbye.

Downstairs she found Rory and Liberty in the kitchen—which was now free of all her destruction. Ian must have cleaned it up.

"You're really leaving?" Liberty slid off the stool she was sitting on.

"Yeah, but I'm not going far." She still had her place to go back to. The only reason she'd come here was be-

242 | KATIE REUS

cause of her crazy family. Bo had insisted she stay with him since his place was safe, protected. Staying here wasn't worth the pain. "I'll leave my cell phone number. If you need anything, just call me. It doesn't matter for what. Even just to hang out." The little time she'd spent with the human, she found she really liked her.

Liberty nodded, but then jumped at a slamming sound.

Nyx turned to find Bo storming into the kitchen, looking pissed. *At her!*

Just like that Ian, Rory and Liberty scattered.

"What you saw isn't what you think," he snarled, advancing on her before she could think about moving. He grasped her upper arm, not hard, but with enough pressure that she couldn't tug away without hurting herself. He kept moving until she backed up against the kitchen counter with nowhere else to go.

Angry that he was trying to use his bigger size against her, she thumped him on the chest with one of her hands. "I didn't see you kissing two *naked* females?"

"No! I kissed the top of their heads, yes—"

"While they were naked! In one of your private rooms!" She couldn't stop yelling now if her life depended on it.

"Damn it, woman! Let me explain." He leaned down, his amber eyes burning bright. "It was Janae and Myla—"

It was like a dagger pierced through her chest. Nyx genuinely liked the two females and as far as she knew they'd never slept with Bo. Until now.

"No! I can see what you're thinking. I didn't fuck them. I've never fucked them. Don't even let your mind go there. I was headed out to catch a flight to London when one of my guys told me Myla was attacked. I was just checking on them. They were both crying so I hugged them, comforted them. That's it."

"Wait... London?"

"Yes, to drag you back home."

Nyx felt some of her steam start to fade, but not much. She wasn't sure she believed him. "How'd you even know I was there?"

He leaned closer so that their noses were almost touching. "Because from the moment you left I called in every favor I had to find you. Drake's mother knew where your father was."

Guilt suffused her as all of his words hit home. There was no way he could know where she'd been unless he was telling the truth. He would have definitely had to make a lot of calls to find out. Which meant he wouldn't have had time to get naked with two females. And... he'd been completely dressed. She winced at the way she'd overreacted. He wasn't lying and the way he'd been holding the females in the room hadn't been exactly sexual. She'd just seen the naked skin and heard him murmuring and had sorta lost it. "You didn't promise anything to anyone, did you?"

"No," he gritted out. "Arya told Drake and Victoria... Shit, they were on their way to pick me up from the club." Growling, he leaned back and rubbed a hand over the back of his neck. "I've gotta tell V I left."

"What?"

"Victoria and Drake were going to head to London with me in the Stavros pack's private plane."

Nyx swallowed hard, starting to feel really, really awful. He'd been trying to find her and she'd totally overreacted. "Is Myla okay?"

"Yeah, she's okay. She and her mate are."

She placed a tentative hand on his chest, wondering if he'd even accept her touch. She should have trusted him. "I'm sorry, Bo. I just saw... and I thought..." Ugh, she didn't even want to say it.

"It fucking hurts me that you'd think that about me!" Now he was the one shouting, but there was such a raw vulnerability in his voice and on his face that it shredded her. "I would never cheat on you. I'd rather cut off a body part than touch another female like that."

"I know. I should have trusted you more. I'm so sorry." She let her hand drop as more panic assaulted her. What if she'd committed some relationship sin? What if he didn't forgive her—

Bo's mouth crushed over hers, hungry, demanding.

Nyx grabbed hold of his shoulders and leaned into the kiss. She knew they still needed to talk, should definitely talk... but he tasted so good, felt so good as she pressed her body against his.

His tongue teased against hers, the erotic little strokes making her melt against him. Still high on the emotions from earlier, she felt more than just relief that she didn't have to leave, to walk away from Bo. She couldn't even put into words the emotions racing through her right now. She was glad he wasn't holding it against her that she'd freaked out.

Bo groaned into her mouth as he grabbed her by the hips. He pulled back, nipped her jaw a little harder than she'd expected. "You're never fucking leaving me again." The soft growl against her skin reverberated through her.

"No."

"I love you," he snapped out, the words giving her whiplash.

She froze, her fingers digging into his shoulders. Breathing hard, she looked at him, wondering if he'd just said it in the heat of the moment. "What?"

"I fucking love you." The words were almost a snarl.

"Why do you sound angry about it?"

"It's confusing! I never thought... I didn't think I was capable of feeling this much for someone. I'm a half-demon! If I lose you..." Stark terror filled his gaze as he trailed off.

She cupped his cheeks hard. "I love you, Bo. And I'm not going anywhere." Deep down she knew she could trust him. She *did* trust him. She'd worked with him for a little while now and she'd never had that reaction to seeing him with females hanging on him. But she'd been feeling raw after dealing with her father. Still, it wasn't

246 | KATIE REUS

an excuse. "And I really am sorry I overreacted. I do trust you." She planned on showing him, not just telling him.

His mouth was on hers again, energy humming through him as he held her tight to him.

Feeling frenzied with the need to have his skin against hers, she tore at his shirt, shoving it up until he thankfully took over. Some distant part of her brain told her to hold on, that they should go upstairs. But screw it.

The place was big and the others had fled the kitchen earlier. Nyx wasn't waiting to have Bo. She felt a sort of mating heat she'd heard shifters talk about. The thought of anyone touching him made her crazy and the thought of him *not* being inside her made her equally so. Or maybe it was wishful thinking. Whatever it was, she felt positively crazed to feel him inside her, pushing deep, over and over.

She wanted him to claim her with an urgency she didn't quite understand. Before his shirt had hit the ground, he grasped the hem of hers, had it pulled over her head.

"Upstairs or here?" he demanded, slicing her bra free with one of his talons.

She hadn't even realized he could unsheathe them in his human form. Before she'd blinked, he'd retracted it. "Here."

In response, he dipped a head to one of her breasts, sucked her nipple hard. Heat flooded between her thighs as he teased the hard bud with his tongue and teeth. Her clit pulsed as her nipples beaded even harder.

She grappled with his pants. This time was going to be hard and fast. He'd been so careful with her last night. Every time they'd come together she'd wondered if he'd been holding back. At least a little bit.

There was no room for that now.

His hands were all over her, stripping her down to nothing in seconds, before she'd managed to even get his pants off.

Breathing hard, he looked down at her, his expression harsh, hungry. "I want to mate with you."

It didn't come out as a question, but she saw it in his eyes. She didn't know how half-demons mated though. Or if he just meant in the general sense. "Me too." A small part of her wondered if it was too soon, but she knew herself, knew there wouldn't be another male for her.

She felt Bo in her bones, in her blood.

"I have to mark you." The words were a savage growl.

She just nodded. The most primal part of her wanted Bo's mark on her, whatever it might be. She wanted the world to know he'd claimed her. "Do it."

Before she realized what he intended he flipped her around, the threads of his control completely shredded away as he bent her over the counter. She felt exposed, a little vulnerable, but she knew Bo would never hurt her.

After today she realized that if she was all in, she *had* to trust him. Had to let stuff that didn't matter go. The past didn't matter, just the way he'd always treated her.

From the very beginning. From the moment she'd walked into his club she'd felt that sizzling, instant attraction.

But it had blossomed into so much more. His protectiveness of her had been what had won her over. She'd never had anyone care about her the way he did.

She'd do anything for this male.

"You're so fucking beautiful." Again, his words were savage, as if they'd been ripped from him.

She loved that at his core he wasn't polished, that everything was raw and primal. That was the way he made her feel, stripped down until he saw every part of her.

His chest pressed against her back as he held her against the counter, pinning her in place. Cool air rushed over her breasts. When he slid a hand around her middle, moved down, down... She sucked in a breath as he stroked his middle finger over her clit.

He'd learned her body so fast, knew how to make her crazy.

Right now she ached for him. She tried to push back against him, but he was immobile. Her inner walls ached, empty, needing to be filled by him. When she tried to move her hips again, he grabbed onto one, held her firm.

A shudder racked her, his display of domination waking up something inside her. Though she wanted to writhe against him, she stopped moving.

He nuzzled the side of her neck as he continued stroking her. The feel of his teeth oh-so-gently raking against her skin as his wicked finger pushed her closer and closer to climax had all the muscles in her body pulled taut.

"I'm close," she rasped out even though she figured he already knew.

His erection was heavy against her back. All she wanted was for him to push into her, to claim her.

She cried out as her climax punched through her, the first wave of release sliding out to all her nerve endings. Before she could draw in a breath, he pulled back, thrust into her.

She arched against the counter, melding back into him as he pushed harder, faster, drawing out her orgasm with a sweet intensity she could hardly stand.

He growled against her neck, murmuring words she could barely understand as his finger continued tormenting her.

It was almost too much. She gripped the countertop, her fingers flexing against it until it cracked under the pressure. She was vaguely aware that she'd already broken most of the cabinets in his kitchen, but couldn't find it in her to care.

He certainly didn't seem to.

"Nyx." Her name on his lips completely shredded her. The way he said it was a mix of hunger and devotion.

When his teeth scored her neck, she jerked against him in surprise. He'd told her that he had to mark her though, she should have expected the teeth.

The brief bite quickly gave way to pleasure until it turned into a buzzing sensation against her neck. She wasn't sure what she'd expected, but this euphoric feeling of completely belonging to another being made everything inside her settle.

Closing her eyes, she lost herself to him as he let out one last growl, completely emptying himself inside her. She wasn't sure how much time passed, how long they lay slumped over the counter.

The male was still half-hard inside her and growing when she found the energy to push up. "Uh, uh. Second round's upstairs," she murmured, finally taking in the destroyed kitchen.

Groaning, Bo pulled out of her. Before she could blink, everything was back in its proper place.

She turned into him, wrapped her arms around his neck. "I like that position."

The grin he gave her was trademark, wicked Bo. "Me too." His gaze drifted down to her neck, his expression going almost unreadable.

"What?" She lifted a hand to where he'd bit her. She couldn't even feel it anymore.

"I... wasn't sure if I did it right. I just went with my instincts." Reaching behind her, he snagged a stainless steel toaster and held it up.

Nyx's eyes widened as she saw the little swirling design of symbols exactly like the ones on his chest when he'd been in his other form. It was a small, circular tattoo on the back of her shoulder. "It's beautiful," she breathed, running her fingers over it.

"It's... a symbol of my lineage. You're sure—"

"I love it." She held onto his cheeks, made him look down at her. The worry she saw there made her want to hunt down his father and end the guy. Because she knew that's where Bo's fear came from. He was afraid she'd care that she was tattooed with his family mark. "I don't care who your father is. This symbolizes you, us."

Relief bled into his amber gaze. "I don't know what I did to deserve you."

"Right back at you." A healthy dose of guilt invaded her veins, dimming some of her pleasure. "And I really am sorry about—"

He shook his head, his expression fierce. "From this point forward, only trust between us. No matter what. I'll have your back—"

"And I'll have yours." A sense of peace and belonging flooded her as he pulled her into his arms.

This was definitely the male for her. She was never letting him go.

* * *

"It's finally quiet," Liberty murmured, a smile teasing her lips as a movie played on the huge television in Bo's game room.

252 | KATIE REUS

The sight made everything in Rory go still. He'd been worried the sounds of sex might upset her so he'd been trying to distract her with mindless entertainment. "Yeah. Probably not going to be eating in the kitchen anytime soon."

She snickered and looked between him and Ian, who was on the shorter couch across from them. His brother was stretched out, seemingly relaxed but Rory knew better. His brother had been tense ever since they'd come to this realm. He hadn't come out and said it, but Ian seemed to be worried about Rory. He knew it was because of his interest in Liberty, but he wasn't sure why that would be a problem with his brother.

"How is it that you guys just found out you have a brother and sister anyway?" she asked, reaching for a bowl of M&Ms on the wood and glass table.

Rory cleared his throat, not wanting to talk about his father at all. Especially considering Liberty had suffered at the hands of half-demons.

"Our father got around," Ian said dismissively.

"Oh." She turned back to the screen, munching on her snack and thankfully, relaxed.

She'd woken up last night because of a nightmare and had reached for him, burying her face in his fur. He'd been in his wolf form, something he was pretty sure seemed to comfort her. He doubted she'd be okay with him sleeping in her bed otherwise.

After a few minutes Ian stood, stretching. "I'm gonna call Cynara, see if she's still out at Bo's place. It's pretty early. You guys want to come with?"

It was slight, but Liberty stiffened. "I'm okay here, but you should go," she said to Rory.

He shook his head. "I'm good."

Ian just nodded and left, but Liberty was still watching him, her expression unreadable.

"What?" he asked.

"You don't have to babysit me."

He just snorted, kicked his feet up on the table. "I know," he said, snagging the bowl from her.

She blinked in surprise, then grinned as she reached for it. "Hey, get your own bowl."

"Pretty sure I just did." But he set the bowl between them, tried not to notice when she scooted a little bit closer to him.

Her scent drove his wolf side crazy. When she tentatively reached for the bowl, something flickered across her face. Fear. It was so fleeting, but it punched into him as if someone had physically hit him.

"I'd never hurt you," he blurted before he could stop himself. He'd wanted to keep things casual tonight. Especially after her nightmare last night.

"I know," she said after a long moment. "My heart knows, anyway. I... I didn't get to eat whenever I wanted. Back in that place. When I'm around you, I feel caught between the girl I was before and who I am now. And I'm not really sure why I'm so comfortable with you. It's scary all by itself. For so long I was afraid every second of every day. I was even afraid to go to sleep because I never knew when he'd be back. I just *knew* that he would return. It didn't matter how many times I escaped. He always brought me back." The words poured out of her in a rush. "The really bad part is, I was actually afraid something would happen to him because..." She swallowed hard, but kept his gaze.

Rory didn't move, didn't say a word. He was afraid if he did that she'd stop talking. So he just sat and listened, his heart pounding.

He could see a thin film of sweat on her forehead as she continued. "He didn't share me with the others. Not that it's much better, but... I know what happened to the other women was bad. Worse than me. If he'd died, I'd have been fair game." She closed her eyes then, looked away.

Fuck. His wolf and demon snarled, slashed at him. He needed to destroy something, to make this better for her. Nothing could do that though. He wanted to reach out and comfort her, but didn't want to startle her. "I buried the females, your friends, when I returned to the campsite." He hoped that gave her a little comfort.

"They weren't my friends." Her voice was cold, icier than he'd ever heard it. It was as if something had shifted inside her. "But thank you." When she looked back at him, she was paler than she'd been even a few minutes ago. "I think I'm going to head to my room."

He stood on instinct, because she wasn't going anywhere without him.

Her lips pulled into a thin line as she followed suit. "Don't feel like you have to—"

"I don't do anything I don't want to." His words were abrupt, but true. He was here because of her. That wasn't going to change anytime soon. "If you don't want me around, I'll... give you space." Rory had to force the words out. Because the thought of being away from her, even being separated by a door, didn't sit well with him.

She wrapped her arms around herself, that invisible wall in place between them. "I feel safe when you're with me. I just don't want you to feel obligated to look out for me." When he started to protest again she shook her head. "I'm just saying, when you change your mind, when... you want space, take it. I won't be an obligation to anyone. Okay?"

"I'm going to say yes because I know it's what you want to hear, but I'm not going to change my mind." That he knew without a doubt. His wolf had completely accepted her. It was one of those rare things he'd heard about happening to his kind.

She watched him with a mix of wariness and hope. "You and your brothers are so different than the males from that... hell."

He wasn't going to tell her that the real Hell was a whole lot worse. "Yeah. Does it bother you, what I am?" He braced himself for her answer, knowing it was realistic for her to be disgusted by him after what she'd been through, but—

Her brow furrowed. "If you mean because you're half-demon too, then no. Humans do messed up stuff every day. Truly evil things I can't wrap my mind around. But they also do really amazing things as well. You guys saved me and you... killed everyone." She swiped away a few tears as they rolled down her cheeks, looked away. "For that I'll always be grateful."

He wanted to brush away the wetness on her cheeks, to tell her that he didn't want her gratitude, but he held back. He was just glad she'd opened up to him. It was a start.

He wasn't sure what she needed to do to get on the road to recovery but he knew he needed to figure it out. Protecting her, taking care of her, had become the most important thing in his world.

So much so, he didn't think he'd ever be going back to another realm. Not when she lived in this one. Because his wolf knew what she was to him, even if he wasn't ready to fully accept it.

* * *

An odd sense of belonging filled Bo as he stepped into his kitchen to find Rory, Cynara and Ian standing at the center island devouring a pizza. It was close to four in the morning and there were three empty boxes on another counter. Nyx was upstairs sleeping and he'd decided to let her rest instead of waking her up for another round when he couldn't go back to sleep.

"You guys are freaking animals," he murmured. "Ever heard of plates?"

Cynara snorted and picked up another piece. "Grab some before it's all gone." He could see from her brighter-than-normal gaze that she'd definitely gone back to drinking tonight.

Despite what he'd said, he didn't get a plate, just snagged a paper towel and a couple pieces of the meat lovers pizza. After the last few hours with Nyx he needed to refuel his energy. "You guys just get in?" he asked Ian and Cynara.

"Yeah. I might have gotten into it with a couple feline shifters at the club," she muttered.

"Why?" he asked.

When she didn't answer, he looked at his half-brother. Ian, who obviously knew what had happened, shoved the pizza in his mouth when Bo looked at him.

"Come on, what's going on with you?" Normally his sister was the epitome of calm. She was definitely more level-headed than him. Always had been.

Shoving her half-eaten slice away, she sat on one of the stools. "It's stupid. I just got a call from an old friend that my ex is mated—to another old friend." She shrugged, the action jerky. "I hate that bastard, but... I don't know, it just shocked me I guess."

Rory let out a low growl. "Whoever he is, he's not good enough for you."

"Especially not that dick," Bo said, since they'd never met the guy.

Ian frowned. "Should we kick his ass? I think that's what brothers are supposed to do. And I could use a good fight."

Cynara laughed, most of the tension seeming to ease from her shoulders. "No one is kicking anyone's ass. I feel like I should send his mate a sympathy card," she muttered, sarcasm lacing her words. "He freaking stole from me when we broke up," she added.

Bo went still at the revelation. "What?"

"Yeah, I didn't tell you back then because I knew you'd probably kill him."

"I'm surprised *you* didn't." Cynara didn't have a high tolerance for bullshit. From what Bo knew she'd caught the male cheating on her and had kicked him to the curb. Even though his true nature had been revealed she'd still mourned their breakup for months.

"I thought about it, but it would have meant hunting him down. He headed to Europe after we broke up. He didn't take that much money and the male isn't worth it."

Bo had a feeling her mood had more to do with the female her ex had mated with than anything. He wouldn't ask for the name yet though. Cynara didn't have many people she considered friends so it would bother her that someone she considered one had mated with such a loser, someone she'd once thought she loved.

"I'm with Ian on this." Rory picked up another slice. "We'll pay him a little visit when the time is right."

"I can't tell if you're being serious." Cynara looked between the three of them as if they'd lost their minds.

Bo just shrugged. He'd wanted to hurt the guy years ago but hadn't because Cynara had asked him not to. "If he's ever in this territory, he's fair game."

"Maybe we can get him down here of his own free will." Ian grinned wickedly.

"You guys are totally psychotic." Cynara shook her head at them, but her tension was totally gone now. She probably thought they were kidding anyway.

Bo took another bite of his pizza, surprised at how at ease he felt around Rory and Ian. The four of them standing here, eating food at four in the morning, felt like the most normal thing in the world. For so damn long he'd felt alone. He knew he was lucky he'd had a mother who loved him, who raised him right, but to gain more family after so many years was a gift he was incredibly grateful for.

CHAPTER EIGHTEEN

"Can I ask you something?" Nyx murmured against Bo's chest, her voice drowsy.

The past two days they'd done nothing but have sex. Well, mostly nothing else. Bo had rarely taken a break from work in his eighty years on this realm, mainly because he liked what he did, but he and Nyx deserved the downtime. Truth be told, he couldn't keep his hands off her. It didn't matter that he'd marked her, that she was his, he felt this driving urge to claim her over and over. "Sure." He kissed the top of her head, held her close.

Her naked body was stretched along his and he loved the feel of all that bare skin against his.

"You don't have to answer if you don't want. I just know you spent a lot of time behind the red door. Before." Her tone was neutral.

He inwardly winced, had known this was coming. While he didn't particularly want to talk about it he knew they should get it out of the way.

She looked up at him, her gaze clear. "I just wondered if there was *stuff* you did in those rooms that you might want to do with me."

Oh. He hadn't been expecting that. His dick got hard—harder—at the thought of doing everything he'd been fantasizing about. It was like he couldn't focus on one thing. Fuck. He needed to answer. He cleared his throat. "I want to do anything you're comfortable with. Anything, anywhere. We've got all the time in the world." She'd been a virgin until recently so he hadn't wanted to rush anything. But the thought of tying her up, taking complete control... yeah. That was going to happen soon.

Her mouth tugged into a smile. "Good. Maybe next time we're at work we can christen your office. I've had some dirty thoughts about doing it on your desk."

He groaned, brushing his mouth over hers. He'd never brought a female into his office for sex but for Nyx, he'd definitely make that exception. Over and over.

As another thought occurred to him, he pulled back a fraction, but kept her close. "Are you okay with me still running the club, now that we're mated?"

"Of course. As long as you don't mind me still working there."

The most primitive part of him hated it. "You don't need the money." That much he knew without a doubt. She'd never said how she came to be so wealthy or exactly how much she had, but as the daughter of a goddess, he could figure it out.

She snorted, making little circles on his chest with her fingers almost absently. "Neither do you."

True. He shrugged.

"I started working there because I wanted some experience in the human realm and because I'd heard your club was an all supernatural one. Made it easier to just be myself. I'm not saying I want to work there forever, but right now I'm having fun figuring out what I want to do."

"You're part owner now anyway," he murmured.

"What?" Her hand stilled on his chest.

"You need to sign a few things but I started the process yesterday."

Her eyes were wide. "You didn't have to do that."

"I know. I wanted to. I own a lot of companies, but this one is my favorite and it's where we met. You should have a stake in it too."

"Just when I think you can't get any sweeter." She shifted so that she was on top of him and straddled him.

Shuddering, he raked his gaze over her sleek, naked body. He ran his hands up her hips, over her ribs and cupped her breasts—

A sharp knock on his bedroom door made him freeze. "Bo!" It was Ian.

Someone better be freaking dead. "I'm busy."

"You've got company on your front lawn. Looks like fae warriors."

Nyx moved off him lightning fast. He wanted to tell her to stay put, that he'd take care of this, but knew that wasn't going to happen. It took restraint he didn't know he had not to go all caveman on her. His female was more than capable of taking care of herself.

"Give me a sec," he called out, grabbing a pair of discarded pants as Nyx dressed in jeans and one of those filmy, flowing tops.

He grabbed a gun from his closet, tucked it in the back of his pants. Then he pulled a blade from one of his drawers, kept it at his side. He preferred to fight hand-to-hand in combat, but sometimes weapons were unavoidable.

"It could be my father," Nyx murmured, pulling the door open. Her expression was apologetic.

"If it is we'll deal with it," he said. Then to Ian. "How many?"

His brother, dressed in combat gear, already had his talons unsheathed on one hand and a wicked-looking blade in his other. His eyes had gone shifter and for the first time since meeting him, Bo had an idea what kind he might be. He pushed back his shock. There'd be time enough to ask the male what he was later.

"I see five. Could be more hiding in the trees. Rory's getting Liberty in lockdown with a full range of weapons right now. He's gonna join us in less than sixty seconds."

"My house is spelled, protected. They won't get in here." Not unless they had dragons attacking it or maybe RPGs might do some damage. He'd worry about those possibilities later.

"Exactly how big is your property?" Nyx asked as they reached the foyer.

"About five acres, give or take. But the gate and walled areas are spelled too. Whatever happens in here, humans won't see any of us. They'll just see my car parked out front." Most of his vehicles were in his garage but he kept one right in front of the main door for a quick getaway if necessary.

"About that…" Ian trailed off.

"They hurt my ride?" He'd left his vintage Mustang out today.

"It's on fire."

Bo's rage burned bright as he yanked open the front door to see five fae males, all in warrior garb on his front lawn, just as Ian had said.

And his car was smoldering with smoke billowing up in black plumes. Yep, someone was going to die. It didn't matter that Bo could fix it. Messing with his ride was a declaration of war. And if these fools thought they could take Nyx, there were no words to describe their stupidity.

"I could just transport them all to Antarctica and leave them." Nyx's voice shook with rage as she stared out at the males.

"You know any of them?" he asked as they descended the steps. The males were tall, with ivory skin, and they all had black hair like her. With supernaturals it could be hard to distinguish true age. They looked to be in their thirties but that could be deceiving.

"Yes," she said through gritted teeth. "The one in the middle is the male I was supposed to be mated to. His name is Vesa." Her words were quiet enough for only him and Ian. "Let me try to talk to them, see what this is about."

Ian just snorted. "It's about you."

Bo didn't fight his instinct as he moved in front of Nyx when they'd rounded the smoking car. "Get off my property, *now*," he snarled, letting his beast show in his eyes.

The tallest of the five stepped forward. He was good looking in the way only supernaturals could be. Classically handsome, with slightly pointed ears. His jaw tightened as he looked first at Bo, then rage flickered across his features when his gaze landed on Nyx.

"This is what you threw me over for?"

"We met one time, dude."

Under any other circumstance Bo would have found Nyx's use of the term "dude" funny. "You don't speak to her. Ever." His voice sounded more animal than human. His demon rippled at the surface, clawing, ready to take over in a second. Unlike shifters, who sometimes struggled with their shifts, his change would be instantaneous.

The male drew out a short sword. "I'm here to fight you to the death. You took my female and I'm here to demand recompense."

Bo rolled his shoulders once. Oh yeah, that was something he could get on board with. "Just you and me. Winner walks away free and clear."

Nyx stepped in front of Bo and faced the male. "Are you freaking kidding me? He didn't take me, you moron. I'm a person, no one owns me. You can work that crap out with my father, but you and I—there is never going to be an us."

"I'm aware of that," the male snarled. "I wouldn't want you now anyway, whore. I still have the right to fight your male."

Nyx took another step forward, the ground beneath them rumbling as she moved.

Bo grabbed her arm. "Let me do this." Because in the supernatural world, power was the only thing that mattered. He needed to kill this male, to show the other fae that he would and could kill for his female. It would send a message.

When she looked up at him, annoyance on her face, he shook his head once. "I know you can kill this male." Or more likely all of them. "I need to do this for us." And okay, for himself.

She paused once, nodded, then stepped back. Worry flickered across her features, but then she masked it. Good, he didn't want her fearful for him. She needed to know he could take care of her, defend her. Even if she didn't need him to. "If any of your warriors try to interfere I reserve the right to kill them," she said to the fae male.

The males just chuckled—as if they thought that idea was hilarious. Bo resisted the urge to smile at their stupidity. They must truly have no idea how powerful she was.

Ian cleared his throat. Loudly.

"Fine, and he reserves the right to kill them as well. Do you agree to the terms?" she demanded, every inch the haughty princess.

Bo loved it.

The fae male nodded. "Agreed. No one interferes. If they do, both sides reserve the right to respond in self-defense."

"Weapons?" Bo asked, figuring the male would want one.

"Blades," Vesa said, withdrawing another short sword.

Bo held up his blade as well as his talons. "These are my blades."

A nod. "Fine."

Nyx grabbed his arm, yanked him down for a quick kiss. "Be careful," she whispered low enough for only his ears.

Just like that the others moved back, giving their leader space. Bo was aware of Ian and Nyx stepping back as well, and even of Rory stepping outside, but he kept the majority of his focus on the dark-haired male.

He'd never battled here, never killed anyone on his home turf. There was a first time for everything.

The male stepped wide, starting to circle him in a dance Bo was familiar with. They would test each other, look for strengths, weaknesses.

Keeping his stance loose, relaxed, Bo rolled his shoulders as he circled with the male.

"I'll kill the female when I'm done with you," the male snarled, moving in a fraction.

Bo knew that wouldn't happen. Mainly because this male wouldn't attempt to kill a fae princess. He knew that much about fae politics. Also because he wasn't remotely strong enough to take on Nyx. But the words set loose his demon half, gave him the freedom to let everything else go and attack.

There was no coming back after threatening a male's mate. Nyx was everything to him, his reason for breathing.

Vesa swiveled his swords with clear skill, the blades whistling through the air with the quick movements.

Too bad for him Bo wasn't going to attack straight on. Though he knew the male expected it.

With about fifteen feet of space between them, Bo took one lunge at the male, inwardly smiled as Vesa moved into his warrior stance, struck out at Bo.

Using all the power in his legs and the momentum of his lunge, Bo sprung into the air, jumping up over the male. As he flew over him, he sliced his talons against Vesa's face and the side of his neck as he passed. Not a killing blow, not even a debilitating one.

But it would piss off the male, make him look weak. Bo didn't want to just kill him, he wanted to send a clear message, humiliate the male before he dispatched him to Hell.

Using his demon speed, Bo sliced at the male's back, shredding through his tunic and digging through skin in rapid-fire slashes.

The male howled, turned with his blades swinging.

But Bo was too fast. He ducked one blade that would have sliced at his head, then struck out at the male's other arm, nearly severing it completely. The short sword fell to the ground with a clanging thunk.

The male screamed, the sound agonizing as he drove his remaining blade at Bo, trying to hit him anywhere.

But the male was too weakened and no match for Bo's fighting skills. He'd known it by the way the male had shown up. If he'd been a true predator he'd have just infiltrated the house or gone after Bo elsewhere. Somewhere like the parking lot of his club. He wouldn't have announced his presence and he sure as shit wouldn't have made a production of burning Bo's car. This male was weak.

Vesa's blade glanced by his ribcage, barely breaking the skin.

Bo ignored the sting, dropped his own blade and released his other talons. With one hand he grabbed the fae's good arm, pulled him close. Simultaneously he shoved his talons into the male's chest. He ripped through bone, flesh and cartilage, and pulled out the male's heart. Vesa's face was frozen in shock, his mouth slightly open, his eyes unblinking with abject terror. Like he was shocked this had been the outcome. Fool.

Blood poured out of the male's chest. Bo held the heart up, then kicked at the male's body, letting his corpse fall at his feet with a resounding thud.

Knowing it was barbaric, he threw the heart at the stunned fae males. He could see murder in their gazes, knew they wanted to attack. But he'd seen enough damn death to last a lifetime. Even if his demon craved the blood and war, he'd give them a chance to leave.

"Your leader wanted this fight, we all followed the rules. I'll allow you to take his body and go. But if any of you attack, we'll kill you and we'll hunt down your families and do the same." The last part was a total lie, but he was done with this. And he didn't want his mate to have to kill anymore either. She'd done enough of that the last week. "And," he didn't look as he pointed behind him, his hand bloody, "what she'll do to you is worse than what I just did." Let them stew on that.

As if on cue, the ground started to rumble again.

Only when the males sheathed their swords did it stop.

Bo stood back, watched as they lifted the dead fae's body and practically raced to the end of his long, winding driveway. If the humans saw that little scene once they left the boundaries of his property, then that was just something he'd have to deal with later if cops came sniffing around his place.

Once he was sure they were gone, he turned to Nyx, a part of him still fearful she'd reject him because of all the violence. The second he focused on her, he knew the fear was unfounded. She rushed at him, uncaring about all the blood as she embraced him.

He held her close, closed his eyes against the top of her head, inhaled deeply. This female meant everything to him.

"I need to go see my father again, make some things clear to him," she finally murmured, pulling back to look at him.

"You're not going without me." That wasn't even up for debate.

"I know."

He pushed out a breath, surprised she wasn't arguing.

"But first we need to see a dragon about a favor." She looked down at her top, now ruined, and winced. "And... we definitely need a shower."

CHAPTER NINETEEN

"Thank you again for coming with me," Nyx said to Arya Petronilla. The female was in full-on warrior mode, as her daughter Keelin liked to put it. Wearing heavy boots, cargo pants, and a fitted long-sleeved T-shirt, she looked ready to kick ass.

"We're happy to." Arya glanced back at her mate, Dragos, and Bo, who were standing behind them on the huge porch with oversized columns. "We'll always be grateful for what you did for Keelin. I... don't even know if we'll ever be able to repay you."

Nyx felt bad for even asking Arya to 'return the favor' but she needed to show her father what would happen if he came after anyone in her life again. Not that she was certain Linos had known what Vesa had done. She was about to find out though.

"Let me try again," she said, ready to knock on her father's door. She wasn't certain he was even in London still. And while she could have just transported directly into his home she'd wanted to do this with a little bit of decorum. He hadn't returned her calls in the last couple hours though so she wondered if he was even here.

"No." Arya stopped Nyx from knocking with a gentle hand. "I scent fae behind the door. They're ignoring us."

274 | KATIE REUS

At that, she just kicked the door, sending the heavy thing flying into the foyer of her father's mansion. It splintered down the middle skidding across the polished marble tile.

Two fae males wearing black slacks, white shirts and black jackets went for their weapons. Guns, not blades. Annoyed, Nyx sent a heavy vase flying off a nearby pedestal, knocking both males on their asses.

As they scrambled to their feet, going for their weapons again, Dragos and Bo moved into action, subduing them on their stomachs. To give the males credit, they didn't whine.

A female stepped out of the entryway of a sitting room, cleaning supplies in hand, her eyes wide.

"Please tell my father I'm here," Nyx said quietly.

The female nodded and hurried away, her shoes soundless as she disappeared down a hallway.

Moments later multiple sets of footsteps snapped against the hallway. When her father appeared with two of the males who'd been at Bo's behind him, she saw red.

"You sent them?"

"No!" he shouted even as the males shook their heads.

"We came here to inform him of what happened," one said, stepping forward. He even bowed his head slightly, as if in respect.

She nearly snorted. Fae and their politics. "Did you know Vesa was coming?"

"No." But something flickered in his eyes. Nyx didn't think her father had been foolish enough to send Vesa directly, but she also didn't think he was completely innocent. As a fae prince he'd know a lot about what his people were up to.

She decided to let it go though. Mostly. "I told you what would happen if you bothered me again."

He flicked a very nervous glance at Arya, but straightened. "I had nothing to do with Vesa's attack on your... mate." He said the word with unconcealed disgust.

"From this moment forward our relationship is severed. If you or any fae come after me or anyone I care about you'll go to war with me and the Petronilla clan." She glanced at Arya, grateful for her and Dragos' presence. It was one thing to make threats, but another completely to bring in this kind of backup. And there were witnesses, which was even better.

Last time she'd gotten her father's promise but they'd been alone. This time, she was getting a contract. Signed in blood.

"Yes, little prince," Arya practically purred, her dragon clear in her gaze. Sweet Lord, the woman was scary. "I'm already annoyed you've been ignoring my phone calls." She made a tsking sound. "So rude."

"I wasn't informed you'd been trying to contact me." He frowned, his expression *almost* sincere.

Arya just lifted a shoulder, smiled, though it was more of a baring of teeth. "It's okay. I destroyed your house in Morocco. There were no casualties. I allowed everyone to exit the premises." She said it matter-of-factly, as if what she'd done by allowing his people to live was so very magnanimous. "I also informed them if they contacted you about it I'd come back and kill them all."

Nyx fought to keep her expression neutral as Linos looked at Arya in horror. "What?"

Arya simply nodded. "It's ash."

Nyx cleared her throat, wanting to stay on topic. "We'll just call that a casualty of your rudeness. I'm here to officially relinquish my title of princess and any claim I have on anything under your lineage. In this realm or any other." She didn't want anything from him anyway, but this was a big thing to the fae. She was giving up her claim to everything her family had to offer, divorcing herself from them. Well, they could keep everything. She had Bo, friends, a real life.

"In exchange we'll sign a contract, in blood, stating that you and all fae will leave me and anyone in my life alone. Anyone and *everyone*. If I've spoken to someone once, they're off limits." She knew it was a ridiculous demand, but wanted to get her point across. "If you don't, you'll deal with me. You've barely seen a fraction of what I can do."

"And she has the full support of my clan. Nyx saved my daughter, Prince Linos. You know how my kind feel about their children. If you are her enemy, you are my enemy."

That simple statement was enough to make Nyx's father nod stiffly. "I agree."

"All of us will sign in blood, including Bo." She looked over at Bo then, who was standing next to Dragos. The two males from earlier were a few feet away, arms crossed over their chests, weaponless. Sulking. "Your agreement will be with the both of us." That way if something ever happened to her, Bo had an iron-clad contract protecting him. She didn't know that he'd even need it, but she wanted it for her own peace of mind. She needed to protect him the same way he wanted to protect her.

"We will sign, then I never want to see your face again. If you come to any of my homes, it will be war. No questions asked," he snapped out, anger and truth in his voice.

Nyx nodded, surprised when she didn't feel an ounce of sadness or pain. Just sweet, sweet, relief that she was about to be completely free from her father's side of the family. Soon, she was going to deal with her mother, but she could only deal with one crisis at a time. "Let's do this then."

"We'll wait out here." Arya made that purring sound again, eyeing the prince as if she wanted to fry him to a crisp then eat him for a snack.

Nyx linked her fingers through Bo's and headed back to her father's office. After this was over, she was taking her mate back to their place and they weren't leaving their bedroom for days. Weeks maybe. She was done with all the drama. She just wanted to hole up with the male she loved and start the life they deserved together.

* * *

Bo kept his arm around Nyx's shoulders as they walked Arya and Dragos out to his backyard. After transporting everyone from London they'd returned to his place because Arya had wanted to speak more with Nyx without nosy fae listening, as she'd put it.

The ancient dragon seemed to have a very soft spot for Nyx since she'd helped save Keelin. Which definitely wasn't a bad thing as far as Bo was concerned. He was surprised she'd even revealed her existence to the fae prince but since she and her mate had woken from their Protective Hibernation apparently they'd decided that their clan—and subsequently others followed suit—had come out to more of the supernatural world. For so long dragon shifters were more myth than anything. Now more and more supernatural beings knew they lived and were very powerful.

"I can just transport you over to Finn's mansion," Nyx said as they reached the middle of the expansive lawn.

"No, we need to spread our wings," Dragos said, the most he'd said at once all day. "But we thank you."

"Yes, thank you. I've had so much fun today. Burning down that obnoxious male's home and scaring him in one of his homes has made me very happy. And now we get to see my sweet son and his mate." Arya smiled, a real one, the action softening the female's face, as she spoke of Drake and Victoria. "Today has been perfect."

"How long are you in town?" Nyx asked.

"A few days maybe. We'll be going back whenever Drake decides to. Plus I'm getting to know my other son's future mate."

"Conall is getting mated?" Bo asked, surprised no one had said anything before now.

Dragos' expression turned wry as he shook his head. "No one is getting mated. My own mate thinks she can meddle in our other son's life."

"It's not meddling. I'm simply getting to know the female he is interested in. She is worthy and strong."

Bo had a pretty good idea who Arya was talking about and agreed. He bit back a smile at the thought that an ancient dragon shifter felt the need to interfere in her Alpha son's life. Arya reminded him of his own deceased mother. Though different species and very different ages, his mother had tried to meddle in his love life until the day she died. She'd just wanted him happy, married. He shelved that thought for now. Thoughts of his mother always left him feeling bittersweet. She'd had a good, long life, and had never blamed him for the circumstances of his birth. If anything, she'd been a fierce protector.

"Oh, tell your brother Ian I'd like to speak to him before we leave. Maybe we can meet at your club for drinks if he's willing to talk to me."

Arya, Dragos and Ian had met briefly when the four of them had returned from London, and Bo had seen the recognition in Arya and Dragos' eyes when they were introduced. It solidified what Bo had suspected about Ian—his other half was a dragon. "I'll let him know. Will tomorrow night work?"

"Yes, thank you."

He nodded once and stepped back with Nyx as they started to undress. They didn't need to stick around for this. Shifters didn't care much about nudity, and while he didn't care either, he didn't want Nyx seeing some other male's junk.

Once inside, he guided Nyx to his office downstairs so they'd have privacy. He wasn't sure where his brothers or Liberty were but he knew they wouldn't be in here.

Nyx sat on the edge of his desk instead of one of the chairs. She wiggled against it, her smile playful. "Is this where we're starting tonight?"

"That's not why I brought you in here, but yes. Definitely." He was already hard thinking about it. He cleared his throat, feeling suddenly nervous as he came to stand in front of her.

Cupping her cheek, he ran his thumb over her soft skin. "I love you, Nyx. More than anything I ever thought possible. I don't think I ever told you, but my mom died of old age, happy and peaceful in her bed. She had such a good life. God knows she deserved it after everything she went through. She wasn't even sad to die, just... worried for me. Worried I'd never find someone to spend my life with. If it wasn't for Cynara, I think I would have been completely lost in the world. At least completely alone." He never opened up like this to anyone, but with Nyx he knew he could be himself. She'd shown that to him.

When she gripped his other hand, laced her fingers through his, some of his tension eased.

He cleared his throat again. "I don't know if it'll matter to you, but I want to get married. I'm half human and I want the symbolism." Being mated mattered to him as well but he needed the marriage too. He needed it all from Nyx.

Her blue eyes brightened. "I've seen a lot of human movies," she whispered. "I think you're supposed to be on one knee."

He was on the ground before she'd finished—and so was she. She slid off the desk and practically tackled him, wrapping her arms around his neck and pressing those perfect breasts against him. God, he loved this woman.

"I'm waiting." Her voice was soft, teasing.

All the tension he'd felt, worried that she wouldn't understand this or want it, dissipated. "Marry me?"

She nodded, grinning. "Definitely."

He slanted his mouth over hers. "I'll get you a ring," he murmured, nipping her bottom lip between his teeth. A really huge one that showed everyone what she meant to him.

"Don't need jewelry, just you." She nipped him back, digging her fingers into his shoulder.

"Please, stop now. I don't want to see this." A familiar, hated voice made him pull back.

On instinct, he shoved Nyx behind him and faced her mother, the goddess of Chaos. He jumped to his feet, ready to attack, when she held up a hand.

"Oh, leave the theatrics to me. I've been waiting for you to call me," she said, her pale blue gaze trailing past him to Nyx, who was now standing next to him.

He resisted the urge to shove Nyx back out of sight. It wouldn't do anything to protect her from this bitch and it would just piss her off.

"Why would I call? I delivered your package." Nyx's voice was carefully neutral.

Her mother's eyes narrowed a fraction. "Did you have fun on your little trip?"

"So it *was* you who sent us there?"

Which was a surprise to absolutely *no one*, but Bo figured Nyx just wanted the confirmation.

"Of course, silly girl." She sniffed haughtily and sat in one of Bo's chairs. Her long, Grecian-style dress rustled as she crossed her legs. "And you're welcome."

All the books on his shelves started to rumble as Nyx stepped forward. "I'm sorry, *what?* You think I should thank you? For what, for almost getting us killed?"

"Don't be dramatic. I sent you there so you'd grow into your powers. You were always asking me to teach you control, so I did."

"You're trying to take credit for…" Nyx scrubbed a hand over her face, looked at Bo. "This is so typical," she muttered, her expression a mix of horror and disbelief.

"I knew you'd be forced to take control," the goddess snapped. "It's the only way any demigods truly learn their powers. I could have shown you some things, but you had to learn by being thrown into the fire. It was the only way you'd ever get a handle on your gifts. Besides, I knew you'd be taking your little half-demon with you to deliver that package. And his brothers were in that realm so you had extra muscle if you choked. I chose that one specifically to send you to."

Bo decided to ignore the 'little half-demon' comment. He didn't give a shit what her mother thought about him. Only that she left as soon as possible. Her presence was hurting Nyx and that was not acceptable. "How did you know my brothers were in that realm?"

The goddess tilted her head to the side a fraction, looking at him as if he was braindead. "I'm a *goddess*."

"You stole that wormhole package from the magic man in New Orleans?" Nyx asked.

She lifted a shoulder. "It isn't as if I killed the male. I let him and his assistant live."

"If you're done, can you please leave? I have nothing further to say to you." Nyx growled, the rumbling finally stopping.

Bo slid an arm around her, not for protection, but just because he wanted to touch her.

Sighing, her mother stood, fluffed out the folds of her dress. "I will never understand you. You should be thanking me. Regardless of your ungratefulness, I also wanted to tell you I'm pleased you stood up to your father. The male he chose would have made a terrible mate. At least you chose wisely with this one." She jerked her chin at Bo without bothering to look at him. "Your children will be very special." Then she was gone, in the blink of an eye, as if she'd never been there at all.

"What did I do to deserve such psychos for parents?" she groaned, burying her face in his chest.

He was going to go back to that whole "children" remark later, but for now he pulled Nyx into his arms, wrapped them tight around her as he kissed the top of her head. "Unfortunately we can't choose." If he'd been able to, he'd have chosen anyone but his own father.

"I know," she muttered, pulling back to look at him. "I'm still sorry I have such a dysfunctional family."

He snorted, kissed the tip of her nose. "Don't apologize to me... Do you know what she meant by special children?"

"No. And she has no prophetic abilities—that I know of." Nyx cleared her throat, her expression nervous. "I know we never talked about having kids but... I'm okay waiting for a while before we even think about it."

"Me too." He couldn't even think about procreating for a really, really long time. Because he was selfish and wanted to spend as much time getting to know his mate as he could before they brought another dynamic into the relationship. Plus, kids freaked him out.

She sighed, relaxing as she leaned into him. "At least we know for certain who sent us to the Hell realm."

"Yeah. We'll have to tell Victoria and Drake their suspicions were right." Not that he'd really doubted Chaos had been behind everything. In the back of his head he'd been worried of the small possibility that an unknown enemy had targeted him instead of her. He'd never admit it out loud, but he was glad they'd been sent there.

Nyx had grown into her powers and he'd met brothers he'd never known he had—and he'd realized he would never stop fighting for the female he loved. He owed the goddess for that.

Right now he didn't want to think about any of that, he just wanted to take the female who'd stolen his heart up to their room and make love to her until neither of them could walk.

As if she read his mind, she jumped up and wrapped her legs around his waist. He caught her, holding onto her as she melded against him completely. Her comment about fantasizing about doing it on his desk came back to him.

Maybe they wouldn't make it upstairs at all.

CHAPTER TWENTY

Two weeks later

"Whatever you're doing, put it down," Ophelia said, her sandals snapping across the kitchen floor as she and Liberty hurried into the room.

Nyx slid her laptop to the side, eyeing the two females. She'd been working on the schedule for the club. In the last couple weeks she'd started taking over some of the admin stuff and found that it fed her organizational obsessiveness. "I'm scared to ask what's going on."

Ophelia was bouncing up and down in her purple Chuck Taylors as she dropped a stack of magazines on the island countertop.

"Bridal magazines?"

"Uh, yeah. You know how long it's been since someone in the pack got married? Normally everyone just gets mated but we are doing this right!"

She didn't bother fighting a grin. "We?"

Ophelia just snorted and picked up one of the magazines. "Since you asked me to be a bridesmaid it's my duty to help. *Ohmygod*, the bachelorette party is going to be amazing."

287

"I'm pretty sure that's the only reason she's excited about the wedding," Liberty murmured, heading to the fridge. She pulled out three bottles of water.

Liberty had started to relax around them the past couple weeks and while Nyx knew she was going to need some sort of counseling, the time she'd been spending with Rory certainly seemed to help. Not to mention Ophelia came by practically every day to check on her. The human still hadn't left the house but it had only been a couple weeks. And she'd at least started spending time on the actual grounds around Bo's house. Progress.

"I don't even want a bachelorette party." She'd seen plenty of human movies and didn't want naked males dancing for her.

"Well you're getting one. Spa day complete with massages, manicures, pedicures, a night out with the girls. It's *happening*," Ophelia said matter-of-factly.

"Oh, well that does sound good. Just no naked males."

Ophelia just snorted again. Which wasn't an answer at all.

Liberty cleared her throat as she sat down at the center island. "I used to be a party planner. Once upon a time."

The room went quiet as Ophelia and Nyx looked at her. In the last couple weeks she hadn't offered much about herself. Nyx figured they could find out about her if they'd tried. Considering Victoria's research skills and all the available information on the internet it would have been child's play, but everyone was giving her time. "Really?"

She nodded. "Yeah, I have a degree in hospitality and business. I... can help with the planning of the wedding if you'd like. I'd love to pay you back for everything you've done."

"I'd love it, but not to pay me back." Nyx knew that eventually Liberty would have to leave the house if she wanted to plan a wedding, but she didn't really care about that as much as she wanted her new friend to start healing and living. This would hopefully give her something positive to focus on. Ophelia had told her that Liberty needed a project or something to get more involved in.

"Have you narrowed down a date yet?" Ophelia asked.

"No, Bo wants next month, which seems insane."

Ophelia was shaking her head before Nyx had finished. "Oh wow, that's way too soon. This is going to be the party of the year."

"Okay, is this really about my wedding or your need to have a crazy party?"

"It can be both."

Before Nyx could respond, Bo and Rory appeared as if out of nowhere. She hadn't even realized her mate was home yet. Smiling, she slid off her chair.

290 | KATIE REUS

He pulled her into his arms and just like that it was as if everything else faded away. "I missed you," he murmured.

"I missed you too."

"You guys are disgustingly adorable. I'm gonna go find Ian. Come find me when you're... done." Ophelia snickered as she headed out and Nyx was vaguely aware of Rory and Liberty leaving too.

She felt a little rude but it was hard to care. "I think we just started planning the wedding. Officially."

He flicked a glance over at the pile of magazines, his lips quirking up. "I talked to Finn today. He said we could use his hotel in November for the venue if we wanted."

So that gave them about seven months. Which was kind of perfect. She didn't want to rush anything but she also didn't want to drag out planning something. "Sounds good to me."

"I'll tell him it's on then." His amber eyes lit up with a wicked glint she knew well.

When she leaned into his familiar, heated kiss she knew there was no one else she could ever spend the rest of her life with. Just a year ago her life had been incredibly different; sheltered, boring and she'd been surrounded by horrible people.

Bo had changed everything and she was glad she was starting the rest of her life with the most honorable male she knew. Now that they'd found each other, she was never letting him go.

Thank you for reading Hunted by Darkness. If you don't want to miss any future releases, please feel free to join my newsletter. I only send out a newsletter for new releases or sales news. Find the signup link on my website: http://www.katiereus.com

ACKNOWLEDGMENTS

I owe a huge thanks to Kari Walker and Carolyn Crane for all your input with this book. It's a lot stronger because of you and I am forever grateful. Joan Nichols of JRT editing, thank you for finding all those pesky little errors. You are wonderful! Thank you to Jaycee with Sweet 'N Spicy Designs for another fantastic cover. To Sarah R., thank you for all the behind the scenes stuff that you do to keep me sane. For my wonderful, wonderful readers, thank you for reading my books! You guys are amazing. I hope you enjoyed Bo and Nyx's story. I'm also thankful that I have such a supportive family who puts up with my erratic writing schedule (and coffee addiction). And last but not least I'm thankful to God.

COMPLETE BOOKLIST

Red Stone Security Series
No One to Trust
Danger Next Door
Fatal Deception
Miami, Mistletoe & Murder
His to Protect
Breaking Her Rules
Protecting His Witness
Sinful Seduction
Under His Protection
Deadly Fallout
Sworn to Protect

The Serafina: Sin City Series
First Surrender
Sensual Surrender
Sweetest Surrender
Dangerous Surrender

Deadly Ops Series
Targeted
Bound to Danger
Chasing Danger (novella)
Shattered Duty
Edge of Danger
A Covert Affair

Non-series Romantic Suspense

Running From the Past
Dangerous Secrets
Killer Secrets
Deadly Obsession
Danger in Paradise
His Secret Past
Retribution
Merry Christmas, Baby

Paranormal Romance
Destined Mate
Protector's Mate
A Jaguar's Kiss
Tempting the Jaguar
Enemy Mine
Heart of the Jaguar

Moon Shifter Series
Alpha Instinct
Lover's Instinct (novella)
Primal Possession
Mating Instinct
His Untamed Desire (novella)
Avenger's Heat
Hunter Reborn
Protective Instinct (novella)

Darkness Series
Darkness Awakened
Taste of Darkness
Beyond the Darkness
Hunted by Darkness
Into the Darkness

ABOUT THE AUTHOR

Katie Reus is the *New York Times* and *USA Today* bestselling author of the Red Stone Security series, the Moon Shifter series and the Deadly Ops series. She fell in love with romance at a young age thanks to books she pilfered from her mom's stash. Years later she loves reading romance almost as much as she loves writing it.

However, she didn't always know she wanted to be a writer. After changing majors many times, she finally graduated summa cum laude with a degree in psychology. Not long after that she discovered a new love. Writing. She now spends her days writing dark paranormal romance and sexy romantic suspense.

For more information on Katie please visit her website: www.katiereus.com. Also find her on twitter @katiereus or visit her on facebook at: www.facebook.com/katiereusauthor.

51778760R00179

Made in the USA
Charleston, SC
03 February 2016